THE ITALIAN'S
CHRISTMAS
MIRACLE

THE ITALIAN'S CHRISTMAS MIRACLE

BY

LUCY GORDON

MILLS & BOON®

Pure reading pleasure™

First published in Great Britain 2008
Large Print edition 2009
Harlequin Mills & Boon Limited,
Eton House, 18-24 Paradise Road,
Richmond, Surrey TW9 1SR

© Lucy Gordon 2008

ISBN: 978 0 263 20582 4

Set in Times Roman 16½ on 19 pt.
16-0409-50298

Printed and bound in Great Britain
by CPI Antony Rowe, Chippenham, Wiltshire

PROLOGUE

THE Christmas lights winked down from the tree, which was hung with tinsel. It was only a small tree, and made of plastic, because the modern apartment of a successful businesswoman had room for nothing larger.

Alysa had always loved her home, its elegance and costliness affirming her triumphant career. Now, for the first time, she sensed something missing. Placing her hand over her stomach, she thought, smiling, that she knew what that something was.

Not that this was a good place for a baby. James's home had more room, and when he knew he was to be a father he would want to finalise the marriage plans that had been vague until now. She would tell him tonight that she was pregnant.

There was one other thing to set out: a small nativity scene, showing Mary leaning protectively over the crib, her face glowing as she watched her child. Alysa had bought it on the way home as an expression of her joy.

Gently she laid it on a shelf, close to the tree so that the lights fell on it, illuminating the baby's face. He looked up at his mother, perhaps even smiling. Alysa tried to dismiss the thought as fanciful, but it returned, whispering of happiness to come.

Why didn't James hurry? He was an hour late, and she loved him so much, every moment in his company was precious. But he would be here soon—very soon.

For the hundredth time she checked that everything was perfect, including her appearance. For once she wore her long hair flowing freely. Usually it was pulled back and wrapped up in a chignon. She kept meaning to cut it short and adopt an austere style, suitable for her job as an accountant. But she'd always deferred the decision, possibly because she knew that her hair was her chief beauty.

She had never been pretty. Her face was attractive but, to her own critical eyes, her features were too strong for a woman.

'No feminine graces,' she'd often sighed. 'Too tall, too thin. No bosom to speak of.'

Her women friends were scandalised by this casual realism. 'What do you mean, too thin?' they'd chorused. 'You've got a figure most of us would die for. You could wear anything, just like a model.'

'That's what I said—too thin,' she'd responded, determinedly practical.

But then there was the hair—rich brown, with flashes of deep gold here and dark red there, growing abundantly, streaming over her shoulders and down to her waist, making her look like some mythical heroine.

James loved her hair, which she'd been wearing down when they'd first met.

'I couldn't take my eyes off it,' he'd told her afterwards. 'One look and I began scheming to get you to bed.'

'You mean you didn't fall in love with my upright character and solid virtue?' she'd teased.

'What do you think?'

How they had laughed together, and the laughter had ended, as it always did, in passion.

'I thought you looked like Minerva,' he'd said

once. 'I've got a picture of her with flowing hair, although not as beautiful as yours.'

'But who was she?' asked Alysa, whose education had been practical rather than artistic.

'She was the ancient goddess of warriors, medicine, wisdom and poetry.'

It had become his special name for her, to be used only in the darkness.

He scowled when she dressed for work, taking up her hair and donning a severe suit.

'It's for my job,' she'd chided him fondly. 'I can't be Minerva for my clients, only for you.'

Once she'd had a couple of inches cut off, without telling him, and he'd been annoyed.

They had actually squabbled about it, she recalled now, smiling.

But tonight she'd taken care to look just as he liked—a slinky dress that took advantage of her slim figure, hair flowing down to her waist so that he could run his fingers through the cascade and bury his face in its perfumed softness. Then they would go to bed, and afterwards, as they lay in each other's arms, she would tell him her wonderful secret.

If only he would get here soon!

CHAPTER ONE

THE cold February sunlight glittered over the place where fifteen people had died in one terrible moment.

Far below, the crowd looked up to where the hanging chairs swung over the top of the waterfall. They were newly installed, replacing the ones that had broken suddenly, tossing the screaming occupants down, down to the churning water, to be smashed on the rocks.

That had been one year ago today, and the crowd of mourners was there to remember the loved ones they had lost. Out of respect for the foreign victims the service was held in both Italian and English.

'Let us remember them at their best—with pride. Let us rejoice in having known them…'

Then it was over. Some of the crowd drifted

away, but others remained, still gazing up, trying to picture the tragedy.

Alysa stayed longer than the rest because she couldn't think what to do or where to go. Something inside her, that had been frozen for a long time, held her prisoner.

A young journalist approached her, microphone extended, speaking Italian.

'*Sono Inglese,*' she said quickly. '*Non parle Italiano.*'

He looked astonished at someone who could deny speaking Italian in such excellent Italian, and she added, 'Those are all the words I know.'

He switched to English.

'Can I ask why you are here? Did you lose someone?'

For a wild moment she wanted to cry out, 'I came here to mourn the man I loved, but who betrayed me, abandoned me and our unborn child, a child he never even knew about, then died with his lover. She had a husband and child, but she deserted them as he deserted me. And I don't know why I came here except that I couldn't stay away'.

But she mustn't say any of that. For a year

she'd allowed nobody into her private grief, hiding behind steel doors that were bolted and barred against the world, lest anyone suspect not only her desolation but also her terrible fear that, if she let go, she might never regain control over the torrents of grief and anger.

Let us rejoice in having known them...

'No, I didn't lose anyone,' she said. 'I'm just curious.'

He was a nice lad. He gave a rueful sigh.

'So you can't point anyone out to me? Nobody wants to talk, and the only one I recognise is Drago di Luca.'

She jumped at the name. 'Is he here?'

'He's the man over there, scowling.'

She saw where he pointed. Her first impression of Drago di Luca was of darkness. His hair was dark, and so were his eyes, which mysteriously managed to be piercing at the same time. Yet it wasn't just a matter of appearance. This darkness was there inside him—in his mind, his heart, even perhaps his soul. Alysa shivered slightly.

His face seemed to be made from angles, with no roundness or softening anywhere. The nose was sharp and distinctive, the mouth and jaw firm, the eyes ferocious, even at this distance. The whole effect was one of hauteur, as though he defied anyone to dare speak to him.

'You wouldn't want to get on his wrong side, would you?' the young man said. 'Mind you, he's got a lot to scowl about. His wife died here, and the grapevine says she'd left him for another man.'

It took a moment before Alysa could answer. 'The grapevine? Doesn't anyone know for sure?'

'She was a lawyer, and the official story is that she was on a trip to see clients. If anyone dares to suggest otherwise di Luca comes down on them like a ton of his own bricks. He's a builder, you see, takes on big projects—new stuff, restoring ancient buildings, that sort of thing.'

She looked again. Di Luca was tall and powerfully built, with broad shoulders and large hands, as though he personally constructed his projects.

'I can see that people could find him scary,' she mused.

'I'll say. He's a big man in Florence. Someone suggested that he stand for the council and he laughed. He has all the influence over the council that he needs without spending time in meetings. They say he has the ear of every important person in town, and he pulls strings whenever it suits him. I tried to speak to him earlier and I thought he was going to kill me.'

She took a last look at Drago, and was disconcerted when he seemed to be looking back at her. Impossible, surely? But for a moment the surroundings faded to silence and all she could hear was a call that he seemed to be sending to her.

Stop being fanciful, she told herself.

'I must be going,' she told the journalist.

She drifted away, managing to keep Drago di Luca in her sights. She knew his face from a hundred obsessive searches of the internet. James had accidentally let slip that his new lover was called Carlotta. Then he'd clammed up.

Three weeks later the tragedy at the Pinosa Falls, near Florence, in Italy, had hit the headlines and she had learned from a newspaper that he was dead. Going through the list of names, she'd discovered Signora Carlotta di Luca, a young lawyer of great promise. Searching the internet, Alysa had discovered several articles about her, and some photographs.

They'd revealed a dark-haired, vivacious woman—not beautiful, but with a special quality. One picture had showed Carlotta with her husband and child, a little girl about four years old, who bore a strong resemblance to her mother. The man with them had been in his late thirties with a face that Alysa hadn't been able to read—strong, and blank of emotion.

Was he also a brutal husband whose unkindness had driven his wife into the arms of another man, and so to her death? Seeing him today, she could believe it.

The internet had also contained depictions of the accident that no newspaper would have dared to publish—intimate, shocking pictures taken by mercenary ghouls, showing smashed bodies in terrifying detail. One had showed Carlotta and James, lying dead on the ground. James's face had been covered with blood, but Alysa had recognised his jacket.

They'd still been in the chair, leaving no doubt that they had travelled together. She'd just been able to make out that in the last moments before death he and Carlotta had thrown themselves into each other's arms.

Now it was over, she told herself. Ended. Finished. *Forget it.*

One night, as she'd stared at the computer screen, she'd felt shafts of pain go through her like knives. What had happened then had been too fast for her even to call for help. Stumbling to the bathroom, she'd collapsed on the floor and fainted. When she'd come round, she had lost James's child.

Afterwards she'd been glad that she hadn't confided in anybody. Now she could weep in privacy. But the tears hadn't come. Night after night she'd lain alone in the darkness, staring into nothing, while her heart had turned to stone.

After giving the matter some rational thought she'd decided it was for the best. If she couldn't cry now she would never cry again, which was surely useful. When you loved nothing, feared nothing, cared for nothing, what was there to worry about?

With that settled, she'd embarked on the transformation of her life. A shopping trip had provided her with a collection of trouser suits, all stunningly fashionable and costly. Next she'd lopped off the extravagant tresses that had marked her earlier existence. The resulting boyish crop was elegant, but she cared little.

What counted was that it marked the end of her old life and the start of her new one.

Or just the end of life?

Her face too had changed, but in ways she couldn't see. It was tense, strained, so that every feature was sharpened in a way that would have been forbidding if her large eyes had not softened her appearance. They were now her main claim to beauty, and more than one man had admired them, only to find them looking right through him.

She'd thrown herself into her career with renewed fervour. Her bosses were impressed. The word 'partnership' began to be whispered. A year after James's death, she should have completely moved on. And yet…

She wandered slowly back to the water and looked up again to the place where James and Carlotta had swung up high, moments before the cable had snapped.

'Why am I here?' she asked him. 'Why haven't I managed to forget you yet?'

Because he was a ghost who haunted her even now, and in this place she'd planned to exorcise him. Foolish hope.

'Leave me alone,' she whispered desperately, closing her eyes. 'In the name of pity, leave me alone.'

Silence. He wasn't there, but even his absence had a mocking quality.

Beneath a huge tree a stone had been erected, bearing the names of the dead, with James near the bottom. She knelt and touched his name, feeling the stone cold beneath her fingers. This was as close to him as she would ever be again.

'*Sapevi che lui?*'

The voice, coming from behind her, made her turn and find Drago di Luca towering over her, glowering. He looked immense, blotting out the sun, forcing her to see only him.

'*Sono Inglese,*' she said.

'I asked if you knew the man whose name you touch.'

'Yes,' she said defiantly. 'I knew him.'

'Well?' He rapped the word out.

'Yes, well. Very well. Is that any business of yours?'

'Everything concerning that man is my business.'

She rose to face him. 'Because he ran off with your wife?'

She heard his sharp intake of breath and knew that he would have controlled it if he could. His eyes were full of murder. Much like her own, she suspected.

'If you know that—' he said slowly.

'James Franklin was my boyfriend. He left me for a woman called Carlotta.'

'What else did he tell you about her?'

'Nothing. He let her name slip, then refused to say any more. But when this happened—' She shrugged.

'Yes,' he said heavily. 'Then every detail came out for the entertainment of the world.'

The crowd jostled her slightly and she moved away. At once he took her arm, leading her in the direction he chose, as though in no doubt of her compliance.

'Are you still in love with him?' he demanded sharply.

Strangely the question didn't offend her as it would have done from anyone else. Their plight was the same.

'I don't know,' she said simply. 'How can I be? By now it should be all behind me, and yet—somehow it isn't.'

He nodded, and the sight gave her an almost eerie feeling, as though she and this stranger were linked by a total understanding that reduced everything else to irrelevance.

'Is that why you came?' she asked.

'Partly. I also came for my daughter's sake.'

He indicated the child standing a little way off with an elderly woman who was leaning down, talking to her. It was the same child who'd been in the picture, a year older.

As Alysa watched, the two moved across to where the flowers lay, so that the little girl could lay down her posy in tribute. Looking up, she saw her father, and she smiled and began to run towards him, crying, 'Poppa!' At once he reached down to pick her up.

Alysa closed her eyes and turned slightly. When she opened her eyes again the child would be out of her sight line. Something was happening inside her, and when it had finished she would be all right. It was a technique she'd perfected months ago, based on computer systems.

It started with 'power up' when she got out of bed, then a quick run-through of necessary programs and she was ready to start the day. A liberal use of the 'delete' button helped to keep things straight in her head, and if something threatened her with unwanted emotion she hit the 'standby' button. As a last resort there was always total shut-down and reboot, but that meant walking away to be completely alone, which could be inconvenient.

Luckily, standby was enough this time, and after a moment she was able to turn back and smile in a way that was almost natural. She could do this as long as she aimed her gaze slightly to the right, so that she wasn't looking directly at the child.

Drago was absorbed in the little girl, whom he was holding up in his arms. Alysa marvelled at how his face softened as he murmured to his daughter, words she could not catch.

The woman spoke in Italian. Alysa picked up *'introdurre'*, and guessed it meant 'introduction'.

'I am Signorina Alysa Dennis,' she said.

The older woman nodded and switched to English.

'I am Signora Fantoni, and this is my grand-daughter, Tina.'

Tina had been watching Alysa over her father's shoulder, her eyes bright. Now Drago set her down and she immediately turned to Alysa, holding out her hand, speaking English slowly and carefully.

'How do you do, *signorina*?'

'How do you do?' Alysa returned.

'We came here because of my mother,' the child said, like a wise little old woman. 'Did you know someone who died?'

Beside her, Alysa heard Drago give a sharp intake of breath, and her heightened sensitivity told her everything.

'Yes, I did,' she said.

Incredibly she felt a little hand creep into hers, comforting her.

'Was it someone you loved very much?' Tina asked softly.

'Yes, but—forgive me if I don't tell you any more. I can't, you see.'

Without looking at Drago, she sensed him relax. He'd been afraid of what she might say in front of his little girl.

Tina nodded to show that she understood, and her hand tightened on Alysa's.

'It's time to go home,' Drago said.

'Yes, I'll be leaving too,' Alysa agreed.

'No!' Drago rapped out the word so sharply that they stared at him. 'I mean,' he amended quickly, 'I would like you to join us tonight, for supper.'

His mother-in-law frowned. 'Surely a family occasion—'

'We all belong to the same family of mourners,' Drago said. *'Signorina*, you will dine with us. I won't take no for an answer.'

He meant it, she could tell.

Drago stroked his daughter's hair. 'Go ahead to the car with your grandmother.'

Signora Fantoni glared, silently informing him of her disapproval, but he ignored her and she was forced to yield, taking Tina's hand and turning away.

'Poppa,' Tina said, suddenly fearful. 'You will come, won't you?'

'I promise,' he said gently.

Relieved, she trotted away with her grandmother.

'Since her mother died she's sometimes nervous in case I vanish too,' he said heavily.

'Poor little mite. How does she bear it?'

'With great pain. She adored her mother. Thank you with all my heart for guarding your words. I should have warned you, but she came to us so suddenly there was no time.'

'Of course I was careful. I guessed you hadn't told her very much.'

'Nothing. She has no idea that Carlotta had left us. She thinks her mamma had to go away to visit clients, and was on her way home when she stopped off at the waterfall. If she hadn't died, she would have been home next day. That's what Tina believes, and what I want her to believe, at least until she's older.'

'Many mothers would have taken their child with them,' Alysa mused.

'Yes, but she abandoned hers, and that's what I don't want Tina to know. Even my mother-in-law has no idea. She too thinks Carlotta was on a business trip and meant to return. Why should I hurt her with the truth?'

'No reason, so it's better if I don't dine with you.'

'Not at all. I trust you. You've already proved that I can do so. You understood everything at once. Shall we go now?'

But suddenly Alysa's alarm bells were ringing. This man was dangerous to her precarious peace. How dared he take her consent for granted? She should run away fast, take the next plane back to England and safety.

'Look, I'm sorry,' she said. 'But I never agreed to this. I have to go home.'

'Not before we've talked,' he said firmly.

Her anger rose.

'Don't try to give me orders,' she flashed. 'We've only just met, and you think you can dictate to me? Well, you can't. I'm going.'

She tried to turn away but he gripped her arm.

'How dare you?' she snapped. 'Let me go at once.'

He gave no sign of obeying her demand.

'Only just met,' he scoffed. 'You know better than that.'

She did, and it was like a blow to the heart. They had known each other only a few minutes, yet their shared knowledge gave them a painful intimacy, isolating them together, facing the whole world on the far side of a glass barrier.

'When you saw me across the water,' he grated, 'you knew who I was, didn't you?'

'Yes.'

'How?'

'I researched your wife on the internet, and you

were part of what I found. Somehow I just had to find out about the woman James left me for.'

'Yes, you *had* to find out. I felt the same, but for me there was no way to do it. I knew nothing about the man she went away with, except his name, and that led nowhere. You've been able to answer some of your questions, but can you begin to imagine what it's like for me, never to be able to find a single answer?

'In there—' he stabbed his own forehead '—there's a black hole that I've lived with for a year. It's been like standing at the entrance to the pit of hell, but I can't see what's there.'

'Do you think I don't know what that's like?'

'No, you *don't* know what it's like,' he raged. 'Because the torment springs from ignorance, and you've managed to deal with your ignorance. But I've lived with mine for a year and it's driving me crazy.' He shuddered then seemed to control himself by force. 'You're the one person who can free me from that horror, and if you imagine that I'm going to let you go without—without—'

It was harsh, almost bullying, but beneath the surface she could feel the desperate anguish that possessed him, and her anger died. So he was ill-mannered—so what? When a man saw his last hope fading, he would do anything to prevent it.

Slowly his hold on her arm was released. 'Please,' he said. *'Please!* You and I must talk. You know that, don't you? You know that we *must*?'

She'd fought his bullying, but his plea softened her.

'Yes,' she said slowly. 'We must.'

Why should she flee? There was no safety anywhere, and in her heart she knew that this was why she had come here—to meet this man, and learn from him all the things she didn't really want to know.

'Come on, then.'

'Only if you let me go. I've said I'll come with you, and I'll keep my word, but if you continue to try to push me the deal's off.'

Reluctantly he released her, but he watched closely, as though ready to pounce if she made a wrong move. His nervous tension reached her as nothing else could have, softening her anger. Wasn't his state as desperate as her own?

His limousine was waiting for them, chauffeur in the driving seat. But Tina and her grandmother were standing outside, watching for his return, the little girl bouncing as soon as she saw him.

'I suggest you sit in the front,' Drago told the woman, and she did as he wanted, leaving him to open the rear door for Alysa and join her with Tina.

'The drive will take about an hour,' Drago said. 'We live just outside Florence. Where are you staying?'

She named a hotel in the centre of town, and he nodded. 'I know it. I'll drive you back there later tonight.'

She spent most of the journey looking out of the window as the land flattened out and Florence came into view. Once she glanced at Drago, but he didn't see her. All his attention was for the little girl nestling contentedly against him, as though he was all her world. Which was true, Alysa thought. She wondered how he coped with the child's heartbreaking resemblance to her dead mother.

At that moment Tina opened her eyes and smiled up at her father. His answering smile made Alysa look away. She had no right to see that unguarded look. It was for his child alone.

But it was the little girl's adoring face that

lingered in her mind, and instinctively she laid a hand over her stomach, thinking of what might have been.

Now they were driving through the city and out again, taking a country road leading to a village, then turning into a lane lined with poplar trees. After half a mile the house came into view, a huge, gracious three-storeyed villa stretching wide, surrounded by elegant grounds.

She knew little of Italian architecture, but even so she could tell that the building was several-hundred years old and in fine condition, as though Drago, the builder and restorer, had lavished his best gifts on his home.

The entrance to the house lay through an arched corridor where the walls were inlaid with mosaics, and the ceiling adorned with paintings. At first sight it was so impressive as to be almost forbidding, but as they went deeper inside the atmosphere became more homely, until finally they came to a large drawing-room where Alysa gasped.

Everywhere she saw Carlotta's face. On one table stood a huge picture of her alone, while on the next table another picture showed her with Tina in her arms. The next one showed mother, father and child together. Various other pictures were dotted around the room, plus souvenirs, as Tina eagerly explained to her.

'That was Mamma's medal for winning a race at school,' she said.

'My wife was a fast runner,' Drago explained. 'We always used to say that she could have been an athlete if she hadn't preferred to be a lawyer.'

'She could run faster than anyone, couldn't she, Poppa?'

Alysa saw Drago's suddenly tense face, and realised how cruelly double-edged this remark would seem to him. But he gave his child a broad smile, saying, 'That's true. Mamma was better at everything,' he said with a fair pretence of heartiness. 'Now, we must entertain our guest.'

Tina set herself to do this, the perfect little hostess. If she hadn't been functioning on automatic, Alysa knew she would have found her enchanting, for Tina was intelligent and gentle. When supper was served she conducted her guest to the table, and in her honour she spoke English, of which she had a good grasp.

'How do you speak my language so well?' Alysa asked, for something to say.

'Mamma taught me. She was bi—bi—'

'Bilingual,' Drago supplied. 'Some of her clients were English, as are some of mine. We're all bilingual in this family. Tina learned both languages side by side.'

'Do you speak Italian?' Tina asked her.

'Not really,' Alysa said, concentrating on her food so that she didn't have to meet the innocent eyes that were turned on her. 'I learned a little when I was researching someone on the internet.'

'An Italian someone?'

'Er—yes.'

'Was that someone there today?'

'No.'

'Are you going to see them tomorrow?'

Her hand tightened on her fork. 'No, I'm not.'

'Will you—?'

'Tina,' Drago broke in gently. 'Don't be nosey. It isn't polite.'

'Sorry,' Tina said with an air of meekness that didn't fool Alysa. Even hidden away inside herself as she was, Alysa could see the enchanting curiosity in the little girl's eyes, and understood why Drago was determined to protect her at any cost to himself.

That's how I would feel, she thought, *if I had a*— She blanked the rest out, and fixed her attention on drinking her coffee.

CHAPTER TWO

FOR the rest of the meal Alysa forced herself to act the part of the ideal guest, assuring herself that it was no different from concentrating on a client. You just had to focus, something she was good at.

She became sharply aware of tensions at the table, especially between Drago and his mother-in-law, whom he always addressed as 'Elena'. For her part she looked at him as little as possible, and talked determinedly about Carlotta, who had, apparently, been a perfect daughter, mother and wife. Drago had spoken truly when he'd said his mother-in-law had no idea of the truth—or, if she had, she'd rejected it in favour of a more bearable explanation.

'My daughter's clients had no consideration, Signorina Dennis,' she proclaimed. 'If they had not insisted on her travelling to see them, instead of coming to her as they ought to have done, then she would have been alive now.'

'Let's leave that,' Drago interrupted quickly. 'I would rather Tina forgot those thoughts tonight.'

'How can she forget them after where we have been today? And tomorrow we go to the cemetery…'

Alysa saw Tina's lips press together, as though she were trying not to cry. She put out her hand and felt it instantly enclosed in a tiny one. The little girl gave her a shaky smile, which Alysa returned—equally shakily, she suspected.

This was proving harder than she had expected, and the most difficult part was still to come.

When supper was over Elena said, 'You're looking sleepy, little one, and we have another big day tomorrow. Time for bed.'

She held out her hand and Tina took it obediently, but she turned to her father to say, 'Will you come up and kiss me goodnight, Poppa?'

'Not tonight,' her grandmother said at once. 'Your father is busy.'

'I'll come up with you now,' Drago said at once.

'There's no need,' the woman assured him

loftily. 'I can take care of her, and you should attend to your guest.'

'I'll be perfectly all right here for a while,' Alysa said. 'You go with Tina.'

Drago threw her a look of gratitude, and followed the others out.

While he was gone Alysa looked around the room, going from one photograph to another, seeing Carlotta in every mood. One picture showed her with a dazzling smile, and Alysa lifted it, wondering if this was the smile James had seen and adored. Did her husband still look on this picture with love?

She heard a step, and the next moment he was in the room, his mouth twisting as he saw what she was holding.

'Let's go into my study,' he said harshly. 'Where I don't have to look at her.'

His study was a total contrast—neat, austere, functional, with not a picture in sight. After the room they had just left, it was like walking from summer into winter, a feeling Alysa recognised.

The modern steel desk held several machines, one of which was a computer, and others which were unknown to her, but she was sure they were the latest in technology.

He poured them both a glass of wine and waved her to a chair, but then said nothing. She could sense his unease.

'I'm sorry you were kept waiting,' he said at last.

'You were right to go. I get the feeling that Tina's grandmother is a little possessive about her.'

'More than a little,' he said, grimacing. 'I can't blame her. She's old and lonely. Her other daughter lives in Rome, with her husband and children, and she doesn't see them very often. Carlotta was her favourite, and her death hit Elena very hard. I suspect that she'd like to move in here, but she can't, because her husband is an invalid and needs her at home. So she makes up for it by descending on us whenever she can.'

'How would you feel about her moving in?'

'Appalled. I pity her, but I can't get on with her. She keeps trying to give my housekeeper instructions that contradict mine. Ah, well, she'll ease up after a while.'

'Will she? Are you sure?'

He shot her a sharp look. 'What do you mean by that?'

'I mean the way she tried to stop you going upstairs to kiss Tina goodnight. Tina needs *you*, and Elena wanted to keep you away. Are you sure she isn't trying to make a takeover bid?'

'You mean—?'

'Might she not try to take her away from you—for good?'

He stared. 'Surely not? Even Elena wouldn't—' He broke off, evidently shocked. 'My God!'

'Maybe I'm being overly suspicious,' Alysa said. 'But during supper I noticed several times, when you spoke to Tina, Elena rushed to answer on her behalf. But Tina doesn't need anyone to speak for her. She's a very bright little girl.'

'Yes, she is, isn't she?' he said, gratified. 'I noticed Elena's interruptions too, but I guess I didn't read enough into them.' He grimaced. 'Now I think of it, Elena keeps telling me that a child needs a woman's care. It just seemed a general remark, but maybe…'

He threw himself into a chair, frowning.

'You saw it and I didn't. Thank you.'

'Don't let her take Tina away from you.'

'Not in a million years. But it's hard for me to

fight her when she's so subtle. I manage well enough with everyone else, but with her the words won't come. I'm so conscious that she's Tina's grandmother—plus the fact that she's never liked me.'

'Why?'

'I'm not good enough,' he said wryly. 'Her family have some vaguely aristocratic connections, and she always wanted Carlotta to marry a title. My father owned a builder's yard—a very prosperous one, but he was definitely a working man. So was I. So am I, still.'

'But your name—di Luca—isn't that aristocratic?'

'Not a bit. It just means "son of Luca". It was started by my great-grandfather, who seems to have thought it would take him up in the world. It didn't, of course. They say his neighbours roared with laughter. What took us up in the world was my father working night and day to build the business into a success, until he ended in an early grave.

'I took over and built it up even more, until it was making money fast, but in Elena's eyes I was still a jumped-up nobody, aspiring to a woman who was socially far above him.'

'It sounds pure nineteenth-century.'

'True. It comes from another age, but so does Elena. She actually found a man with a title and tried to get Carlotta to marry him. When that didn't work, she told me that Carlotta was engaged to the other man. I didn't believe her and told her so. She was furious.'

'So you really had to fight for Carlotta?'

'There was never any doubt about the outcome. As soon as I saw her, I knew she was mine.'

'Was', not 'would be', Alysa noted.

'How did you meet?' she asked.

'In a courtroom. She'd just qualified as a lawyer and it was her first case. I was a witness, and when she questioned me I kept "misunderstanding" the questions, so that I could keep her there as long as possible. Afterwards I waited for her outside. She was expecting me. We both knew.'

'Love at first sight?'

'Yes. It knocked me sideways. She was beautiful, funny, glowing—everything I wanted but hadn't *known* that I wanted. There had been women before, but they meant nothing beside her. I knew that at once. She knew as well. So when Elena opposed us it just drove us into an elopement.'

'Good for you!'

'Elena has never really forgiven me. It was actually Carlotta's idea, but she won't believe that. She never really understood her own daughter—how adventurous Carlotta was, how determined to do things her own way—'

He stopped. He'd gone suddenly pale.

'How did you manage the elopement?' Alysa asked, to break the silence.

'I'd bought a little villa in the mountains. We escaped there, married in the local church and spent two weeks without seeing another soul. Then we went home and told Elena we were married.'

'Hadn't she suspected anything?'

'She'd thought Carlotta was on a legal course. To stop her getting suspicious, Carlotta called her every night, using her mobile phone, and talked for a long time.'

So Carlotta had been clever at deception, Alysa thought. She hadn't only been able to think up a lie, she'd been able to elaborate it night after night, a feat which had taken some concentration. The first hints had been there years ago. In his happiness Drago hadn't understood. She wondered if he understood now.

He'd turned his back on her to stare out of the window into the darkness.

Images were beginning to flicker through Alysa's brain. She could see the honeymooners, gloriously isolated in their mountain retreat. There was Drago as he must have been then: younger, shining with love, missing all the danger signals.

Suddenly he turned back and made a swift movement to his desk, unlocking one of the drawers and hauling out a large book, which he thrust almost violently towards her. Then he resumed his stance at the window.

It was a photo album, filled with large coloured pictures, showing a wedding at a tiny church. There was the young bride and groom, emerging from the porch hand in hand, laughing with joy because they had secured their happiness for ever.

Carlotta was dazzling. Alysa could easily believe that Drago had fallen for her in the first moment. And James? Had he too been lost in the first moment?

She closed the book and clasped it to her, arms

crossed, rocking back and forth, trying to quell the storm within. She'd coped with this—defeated it, survived it. There was no way she would let it beat her now.

She felt Drago's hands on her shoulders.

'I'm sorry,' he said heavily. 'I shouldn't have done that.'

'Why not?' she said, raising her head. 'I'm over it all now.'

'You don't get over it,' he said softly. She turned away, but he shook her gently. 'Look at me.'

Reluctantly she did so, and he brushed his fingertips over her cheeks.

'It was thoughtless of me to show you this and make you cry.'

'I'm not crying,' she said firmly. 'I never cry.'

'You say that as if you were proud of it.'

'Why not? I'm getting on with my life, not living in the past. It's different for you because you have Tina, and the home you shared with your wife. You can't escape the past, but I can. And I have.'

He moved away from her.

'Maybe you have,' he agreed. 'But are you sure you took the best route out of it?'

'What the devil do you mean?'

'"Devil" is right,' he said with grim humour. 'I think it must have been the devil who told you to survive by pretending that you weren't a woman at all.'

'What?'

'You crop your hair close, dress like a man—'

She sprang to her feet and confronted him.

'And you call Elena nineteenth-century! You may not have heard of it, but women have been wearing trousers for years.'

'Sure, but you're not trying to assert your independence, you're trying to turn yourself into a neutered creature without a woman's heart or a woman's feelings.'

'How dare you?' She began to pace the room, back and forth, clenching her fists.

'Maybe it's the only way you can cope,' Drago said. 'We all have to find our own way. But have you ever wondered if you're damaging yourself inside?'

'You couldn't be more wrong. I cope by self-control, because that's what works for me. Without it I might have cracked up, and I wouldn't let that happen. So I don't cry. So what? Do *you* cry?'

'Not as much as I used to,' he said quietly.

The answer stopped her in her tracks. It was the last thing she'd expected him to say.

'The emotions and urges are there for men as well as women,' he added.

'Maybe you can afford to give in to them,' she snapped. 'I can't. This is how I manage, and it works fine. I'm over it, it's finished, past, done with.'

'Do you know how often you say that?' he demanded, becoming angry in his turn. 'Just a little too often.'

'Meaning?'

'Meaning that I think you're trying to convince yourself—say it enough and you might start to believe it.'

'I say it because it's true.'

'Then what were you doing at the waterfall today? Don't try to fool me as you fool yourself. If it was really finished, you'd never have come here.'

'All right, I wanted to tie up a few loose ends. Maybe I needed to find out the last details, just to close the book finally. It troubles me a little, but it doesn't dominate me, and it hasn't destroyed me *because I won't let it.*'

But she heard the shrill edge to her own voice, and knew that she was merely confirming his suspicion. He was actually regarding her with pity, and that was intolerable.

'Stop pacing like that,' he said, taking hold of her with surprisingly gentle hands. 'You'll fall over something and hurt yourself.'

She stood, breathing hard, trying to regain her self-control. She wanted to push him away, but the strength seemed to have drained out of her. Besides, there was something comforting about the hands that held her: big, powerful hands that could lift a stone or console a child.

'Sit down,' he said quietly, urging her back to the chair. 'You're shaking.'

After a few deep breaths she said, 'Aren't we forgetting why I'm here? You wanted me to fill in the gaps in your knowledge, and I'll do it, but my feelings are none of your business. Off-limits. Do you understand?'

He nodded. 'Of course.' He managed a faint smile. 'I told you that Elena thinks I'm a man-nerless oaf, without subtlety or finesse, going through life like a steamroller. I dare say by now you agree with her.'

She shrugged. 'Not really. You said yourself, we all find our own way of coping. Yours is different to mine, but to hell with me! To hell with the rest of the world. If it works for you…'

'My way no more works for me than yours works for you,' he said quietly. 'But with your help I might find a little peace of mind. I'm afraid my manners deserted me earlier today.'

'You're referring to the way you kidnapped me?'

'I wouldn't exactly say—Yes, I suppose I did. I apologise.'

'Now that I'm here,' she said wryly.

'Yes, it's easy to apologise when I've got my own way,' he agreed with a touch of ruefulness. 'That's how I am. Too late to change now. And if you can tell me anything…'

'Are you sure you want to know? Learning the details doesn't make it any easier. If anything it hurts more.'

He nodded as if he'd already thought of this.

'Even so, I've got to pursue it,' he said. 'You of all people should understand that.'

'You really know nothing about James?'

'Carlotta rented a small apartment in Florence, but it was in her name with no mention of him on the paperwork. I went over there and found enough to tell me that her lover was called James Franklin, but that was all.'

'No other address?'

'One in London, in Dalkirk Street, but he'd left it shortly before.'

'Yes, that was where he lived when I knew him. Did you discover when the Florence apartment was rented?'

'September.'

'So soon after they met,' she murmured.

'That was my thought too. Their affair must have started almost at once, and the first thing she did was hunt for a love nest. I found it looking oddly bare—very little personal stuff, almost like a hotel room. I suppose they spent all their time in bed.'

'Yes,' she agreed huskily. 'I suppose so. But surely he must have brought some things with him from England?'

'It's a very tiny apartment. They were probably looking for something larger.'

'And his things would be stored in England until he was ready to send for them,' Alysa said. 'Only he never had the chance. I wonder what became of them?' She gave a sigh. 'Oh well!'

'I couldn't find anything on the internet about him. What did he do for a living?'

'Nothing for the last few months. He used to work in a big city institution—that's how we met. I'm an accountant and they hired me. He hated the job—being regimented, he called it. Then he came into some money and he said he was going to fulfil his real ambition to be a photographer. He left the job, bought lots of expensive equipment and started taking pictures everywhere, including several trips abroad. He asked me to go with him, and I promised I would when I could get some time off.

'But that never seemed to happen. I should have gone with him to Florence, but at the last minute I couldn't get away. I had several new clients.'

'And they mattered more than your lover?' Drago asked curiously.

'That's what he said. He said I couldn't even spare him a few days. But I'd worked so hard to get where I was—I knew he didn't really understand, but I never imagined— I thought James and I were rock-solid, you see.'

He didn't reply, and his very silence had a tactful quality that was painful.

'I should have gone with him,' she said at last. 'Maybe no love is as solid as that. So he came to Florence without me, and that's probably when he met Carlotta.'

The picture show had started again in her head, and she watched James's return to England, herself meeting him at the airport although he'd told her there was no need.

Now she noticed things she'd missed at the time: the slight impatience in his face when he saw her, showing that he really hadn't wanted her there. Nor had he been pleased when she accompanied him to his apartment, although he'd cloaked his reluctance in concern for her.

'Shouldn't you be at work? They won't like it if you take too much time off.'

Laughing, she'd brushed this aside.

'I told them I wasn't going back today. When we get home, I'm going to cook you supper, and then… And then, anything you want, my darling.'

'So today your time's all mine?' he'd asked.

Had she been insane to have missed the note of irony?

'When we met at the airport he wasn't pleased to see me,' she murmured now, to Drago. 'Of course he wasn't. He'd met *her*, and his heart and his thoughts were full of her. The last thing he wanted was me. He tried to dissuade me from going home with him.'

'Did you go anyway?' Drago asked.

'Oh yes. I was that stupid. I tried to take him to bed, and believed him when he said he was too tired after the journey. I didn't even get the message when he wouldn't let me help him unpack.'

'We can be frighteningly blind when we don't realise that things have changed for ever,' Drago said quietly. 'And perhaps we fight against that realisation, because we're fighting for our lives.'

'Yes,' she whispered. 'Yes.'

James had put his suitcases in the wardrobe, insisting that he would unpack them later. There had been no need for her to worry herself. But he'd kept out the bag where he kept his cameras.

'I'm dying to see the pictures you've taken,' she'd said, opening the side of one of them, ready to take out the little card that fitted into the computer.

It had been gone.

'I've removed them all,' he'd said quickly. 'If anything happens to the cameras on the journey, at least I've got the cards.'

'But you always keep the cameras with you. You've never bothered taking the cards out before.'

He'd shrugged.

It was obvious now that the cards had been full of pictures of Carlotta, and he'd made sure she wouldn't see them.

Reaching into the bag, she'd found a small metal object, which she'd drawn out and studied curiously. It was a padlock, but unlike any padlock she'd ever seen, with tiny pictures on each side. One side had showed a heart, and the other side depicted two hands clasped. The shapes had been studded with tiny, gleaming stones that had looked as though they might be diamonds.

'How charming,' she'd said.

'Yes, isn't it?' he'd said heartily. 'I thought you'd like it.'

'Is it for me?'

'Of course.'

She'd felt for the key in the rucksack. Then she'd smiled at him, all fears removed.

'I shall keep you padlocked in my heart,' she'd told him. 'See?'

But the key hadn't fitted into the lock.

'Sorry,' he'd said. 'It must be the wrong one.

I'll sort it out later.' He'd kissed her cheek. 'Now I'm going to collapse into bed. I'll call you in the morning.'

That memory returned to her now, but she didn't mention it to Drago, because she didn't know what it meant. James had never given her the right key, and had taken back the padlock in the end.

'When did this happen?' Drago asked.

'About September.'

He nodded. 'Yes, I remember Carlotta suddenly started spending a lot of time away from home. She was gone for a whole week in September, then she was at home for a while. There were weekends, then another week in November. I found out afterwards that she'd spent that week in England.'

'The tenth to the seventeenth?' Alysa asked, dazed.

'Was *he* away then?'

'He said he was. He said he was going to drive north and get pictures of some wild scenery, immerse himself in the landscape, talk to nobody, even me. I tried to call him once but his phone was switched off. Then someone mentioned seeing him near his home in London. I said they were mistaken, but I guess they weren't. He must have spent the week at home—with her.'

'She was more shrewd than him,' Drago said. 'She never turned her mobile phone off. She used to call me every day and talk as though all was well with us.' He drew a sudden, sharp breath.

'Just like the other time, when you eloped,' Alysa said, reading his mind.

'Yes, just like then. It's so easy to see it now.'

'Did you never suspect anything?'

'No. I trusted her totally. I went on being blind right up until the moment when she told me she was in love with someone else, and was leaving me for him. And do you want to hear something really funny? I didn't believe her. I thought it wasn't possible. Not my Carlotta, who'd been so close to me that she was like a second self. Only I'd been deluding myself. There was no second self. I'd been alone all the time and never known it.'

'You felt that too?' she asked quickly. 'That's it exactly—as though you'd imagined every-thing. And suddenly the whole world seems full of ghosts.'

'And you feel as though you're going mad,' he confirmed. 'In a strange way, my other self is you.

I can say things to you that I could say to nobody else, and know that you'll understand them.'

'And even the words don't always have to be said,' she mused. 'It's a bit scary. To me, anyway.'

'You think I'm not scared?' he asked with grim humour. 'Do I do that good a job of hiding it?'

'Not really. Not from me.'

'Exactly,' he said in a quiet voice.

She had a fatalistic sense that she was being drawn onwards by powers too strong for her. She'd neither wanted nor sought this alliance, but there was no escaping it.

CHAPTER THREE

'How did you find out?' he asked.

'I suppose the first hint was at Christmas, although I didn't see it. We were going to spend the time together, and I got everything ready—tree, decorations, new dress.' She gave him a faint smile of complicity, as if to say, 'I do wear them sometimes'. He nodded, understanding.

'Then he rang to say he wouldn't be coming. A friend had suffered a tragedy and was suicidal. James didn't want to leave him. It sounds a weak story now, but it might have been true. At any rate, I trusted him. I suppose you think that sounds stupid.'

Drago shook his head. 'My own credulity strikes me as stupid, not yours. There's no limit to what we can believe when we *want* to believe.'

'Yes,' she sighed. 'And I wanted so much to believe.'

She still couldn't bear to speak of her dead child, but unconsciously she laid a hand over her stomach. Drago, watching her, frowned slightly, and a sudden question came into his eyes.

'How long was he away?' he asked.

'Until the first week in January. I guess he came here and spent time with Carlotta, but she couldn't have seen much of him at Christmas.'

'She was with us on Christmas Day, but the rest of the time she did a lot of coming and going. In Italy we also have another big occasion— Epiphany, January sixth, when we celebrate the coming of the three wise men. Carlotta was there for Epiphany—loving mother, loving wife—' He broke off.

After a moment he resumed. 'She played her part beautifully. When it was over Tina left with her grandmother to visit Carlotta's sister and her family. Elena wanted her to go too, but Carlotta said she wanted to stay with me, that we needed some time together. I think that was one of the happiest moments of my life. I'd seen so little of her, and I was overjoyed that she wanted to be with me.

'But as soon as we were alone she said she was leaving me for another man, and there was no point in discussing it. I'd never heard her sound so much like a lawyer.

'I reminded her that she was a mother, but it was like talking to a brick wall. She knew what she wanted, and nothing else counted. I said I wouldn't let her take my daughter. I thought that would make her stop and think. But I discovered that she'd never meant to take Tina.'

'Would you have taken her back?' Alysa asked curiously. 'Knowing that she'd been unfaithful?'

'It would never have been the same between us,' he said sombrely. 'But, for Tina's sake, I would have tried.'

After that there was silence for a while. Drago got up and poured a couple more glasses of wine, handed her one and sat down again.

'I began to realise that I'd never really known her,' he said. 'She seemed not to understand what she was doing to other people, or care. She kept saying, "We've had a lovely Epiphany. Tina will have that to remember".'

Alysa winced. 'She really thought that would be enough?'

'She seemed to. She said she'd come and see Tina sometimes, as though that settled it. Then she left. When Tina came home I told her that Mamma was away on business, because I still hoped she'd come back, and Tina need never know the truth. But then Carlotta died, and how could I tell her then?'

'You couldn't, of course. But can you keep it a secret for ever? Suppose she hears it from someone else?'

'I know. Maybe one day, when she's old enough to cope, but not yet.'

'I can't understand why she didn't want her daughter.'

'Neither can I. Carlotta kept saying we had to be realistic— Why, what's the matter?'

Alysa had turned and stared at him. 'She actually used that word—*realistic*?'

'Yes, why?'

'Because James used it too,' she said, beginning to laugh mirthlessly. 'When he came home in January he called me to meet him at a restaurant. He kept it short, just said he'd met someone else.

He said it hadn't been working out for us, and we had to be "realistic". Then he called for the bill, we said goodbye and I never saw him again.'

'Like a guillotine descending,' Drago said slowly.

'Yes, that describes it perfectly,' she said, much struck. 'And when the blade had descended it stayed there, so that I couldn't look back beyond it. I knew the past had happened, but suddenly I couldn't see it any more. And when I finally did, it looked different.'

'Oh yes,' he murmured. 'It's exactly like that. And you never heard from him? Not a postcard or a phone call to see if you were all right?'

'His lawyer called me to say James had left some things with me and wanted them back. I packed them up in a box and someone from the lawyer's office collected them.'

Drago said something violent in a language she didn't understand.

'What does that mean?' she asked. 'It didn't sound like Italian.'

'It's Tuscan dialect, and I won't offend your ears by translating.'

'Sounds like some of the things I said in those days.'

'You told Tina that you'd learned a little Italian by researching online. Was that—?'

'Yes. When I was trying to find out about Carlotta I discovered a lot of stuff in Italian newspapers. The computer translated it, but very badly, so I got an Italian dictionary. I worked on it night after night and I suppose I went a bit mad.' She gave a short, harsh laugh, turning to the mirror on the wall. 'Look at me.'

In the dim light the mirror made her eyes seem larger than ever in her delicate face. They were burning and haunted.

'Those eyes belong behind bars,' she murmured.

'Stop that!' His voice crashed into her brooding thoughts, making her jump. 'Stop that right now!' he commanded. 'Don't put yourself down. It's the way to hell.'

'It's a bit late for that.'

'All the more need to be strong.'

'Why?' she shouted. 'Sometimes I'm tired of being strong. I've spent the last year working at that—hiding my feelings, never letting anyone suspect.'

'And what's inside you now?'

'Nothing, but that's fine. I can cope with

"nothing". Don't dare to judge me. What do you think you know about me?'

'I know you're a steely accountant, but as a woman you're settling for a narrow life because you think you'll be safe. But you won't. It's just another kind of hell.'

'Look, I came here to help you—'

'But maybe you need my help too.'

'I don't.'

Instead of arguing, he shrugged and said, 'Let's get some coffee.'

He led her into the kitchen, a shining temple to the latest hi-tech cooking equipment, incongruous against the rest of the house. In a moment he had the coffee perking, and brought some spicy rolls out of the cupboard. He'd made the right move. Alysa felt herself growing calmer as she ate and drank.

'Thank you,' she said as he refilled her cup. 'I don't normally lose my temper.'

'Tonight's been hard on you,' he said. 'I shouldn't really have put you through it, but I'm clutching at straws.'

'We all do what we must to survive. I was never going to let this get the better of me.'

'But you've paid a price.'

'Yes, all right, I have. There's always a price to be paid, but anything's better than giving in.'

'You're a very strong person. I admire that. I've often felt it was getting the better of me.'

'Did you mean what you said about crying?' she asked.

'Yes,' he said quietly. 'I meant it. What about you? You said you never cried.'

'I can't. And, if I could, I wouldn't.'

'How did you get to be so strong?'

'Through my mother. When I was fifteen my father walked out on us, and it finished her. She never recovered. I can still hear her sobbing, night after night. Three years later she died of a heart attack. She had no strength to fight it.'

'Poor soul.'

'Yes, and you know why she went under? Because my father was all she had. She was an actress before she met him—a good one, people said. But she had to choose, and she chose him. She wouldn't take jobs that took her away from him, and in the end the offers stopped coming. She became a barmaid, a shop assistant, any number of dead-end jobs. He left her with nothing. That's where I'm different. When I lost James, I didn't lose everything.'

He gave her a quick look and seemed about to speak, but thought better of it and poured some more coffee.

'Did your father stay in touch?' he asked at last.

'He contacted me after she died, said he thought we could repair the past. I told him to get out of my sight and never come back. And he did. I'll never forgive him for what he did to my mother, and I'll never let myself go under as she did.'

He nodded slowly. 'And you have no other family?'

'My mother has a couple of sisters, but they more or less deserted her when she hit the bad times. I suppose they couldn't cope with her depression, and perhaps I ought to be understanding, but they weren't there when she needed them.'

'Maybe it would have made no difference,' he mused. 'Other people can't always help, unless it's exactly the right person. And you may never meet that person.'

'You sound as though you had a lot of experience with the wrong ones.'

'One or two. It wasn't their fault. They tried to

sympathise over her death, not knowing that the real grief lay elsewhere.'

'How did you hear that Carlotta was dead?'

'From the press. Somebody recognised her body and called me. I don't recall exactly what I said, but I think I recited the line about her being away to visit clients. If I did, I was on automatic. Then there were more calls, as the press began to sniff something out.'

'How ghastly!' she said in genuine sympathy.

'I think I went off my head for a while. I was in a rage—I can be really unpleasant.' He gave a faint, self-mocking smile. 'Though you might not believe that.'

'I'll try,' she said lightly. 'Did you actually hit anyone?'

'There was one moment with an editor—but he gave as good as he got. Then I told him if he slandered my wife I'd have his paper closed down.'

'Could you do that?' Alysa asked, remembering what the young journalist had told her.

'Who knows? I'd have had a good try. But he believed it, and that was all I needed. Are you shocked?'

'No. I've done that too. Not the punch-up, but

making the other side think you're stronger than you are. It's very useful. What about the rest of the press? Did you have to get tough with them?'

'No need. The word got around, and after that nobody would challenge me.' He regarded her satirically. 'I dare say your reputation goes ahead of you as well?'

'Well, I'm in line for a partnership.' She too became self-mocking to say, 'So there are some advantages to renouncing my femininity.'

'Look, I shouldn't have said that. Will you please forget it?'

'Of course.' But it had struck home, and Alysa knew she wasn't going to forget any time soon.

'What about you?' Drago asked. 'How did you hear?'

'I got a call from Anthony Hoskins, James's lawyer. He said he'd been contacted by a man who wouldn't say who he was, but was asking about James.'

'That was me. I found a letter from Hoskins in their apartment. I didn't get anywhere talking to him, so I simply passed his name on to the undertakers.'

'They called Hoskins too, and he called me

again,' Alysa remembered. 'He said they wanted burial instructions. James had no family.'

'What did you tell them to do about the burial?'

'Nothing. I was in a dreadful state, so I said I didn't know him and put the phone down. I never heard any more. I don't know what happened to his body.'

'I can tell you that. He's near the Church of All Angels, the same place where Carlotta is buried. There's going to be a ceremony there tomorrow.'

'I didn't know. I only discovered about today's gathering by accident online. There was no mention of anything else. Do you go to the cemetery often?'

'I take Tina to visit her mother, and sometimes I go to see her alone.'

'You visit her, after what she did to you?'

'I have to. Don't ask me why, because I couldn't tell you. I always look at his stone when I'm there. Then I can tell him how much I hate him. I enjoy that. I only wish I could picture him. When I went to identify Carlotta I made them show me him as well, because I wanted to see his face.'

'What did you think of it?' she asked, almost inaudibly.

'Nothing. It was badly damaged, so I still don't really know what Carlotta saw when she looked at him. But you can tell me. Would a woman think he was handsome?'

'Yes,' she said with a touch of defiance. Something about his tone was making her defensive. 'He was very handsome. Do you want to see?'

He stared. 'You've actually got his picture? You still take it everywhere?'

'No, just here. After all, I came here to remember him. I wanted him to be with me. I suppose that sounds crazy?'

He shook his head. She felt in a compartment of her bag, and offered it to him.

To her surprise he hesitated before taking it, as though at the last minute he was unwilling to face the man his wife had loved. Then he took it quickly and studied it, his mouth twisted, so that his turbulent emotions were partly concealed.

'Pretty boy,' he said contemptuously.

'I suppose he was,' Alysa said. 'I used to be proud to be seen with him, because all the other women envied me. They would try to get his attention and they never did because he always kept his eyes on me. That was part of his charm. He had beautiful manners—until the end, anyway. Maybe that's why I didn't see it coming.'

'Tomorrow I'll show you where he lies, a place where nobody is competing for him,' Drago said with grim satisfaction. 'But I dare say you don't need a grave to tell him you hate him.'

'I don't hate him any more.'

'You're fortunate, then. I don't believe you for a moment, but perhaps even the illusion is useful—until it collapses.'

Once she would have insisted that it would never collapse, but this evening had left her shaken, and suddenly she longed to bring it to an end. If anything brought about the collapse it would be Drago di Luca, with his unnerving combination of ruthlessness and vulnerability.

'It's late,' she said. 'I should be going.'

'I'll drive you. We have to be at the cemetery at noon tomorrow. My car will call for you at eleven.'

'No, please. I won't go to the cemetery. Today was enough.'

'Think about it tonight. I'll call you tomorrow.'

She made no answer and he showed her out into the hall, saying it would only take him a moment to bring the car around. She sat down to wait, so sunk in thought that at first she didn't see the little figure coming down the stairs, and jumped when Tina spoke to her, asking anxiously, 'Is Poppa all right?'

'Yes, of course,' Alysa said. 'Why do you ask?'

'He was unhappy all day.'

'Well, your mother…'

'I know. He's always unhappy about her, but today he was nervous too.' Tina lowered her voice to say, 'I think he's nervous of Nonna.'

'Nonna?'

'My grandmother. She hasn't been very nice to him today.'

There was an almost motherly note in the child's voice. Alysa realised that, while Drago was protecting her, this little creature was protecting him.

He returned at that moment.

'What are you doing out of bed?' he demanded, in a voice in which authority and tenderness were equally mixed.

'I came to see how you were,' the child explained.

'I'm going to drive the *signorina* home, but then I'm coming right back. Now, get back to bed before your grandmother finds out, or I'll be in deep trouble.'

At that moment the sound of Elena's voice upstairs made them all freeze.

Tina reacted like lightning. Reaching up to Alysa's ear, she whispered, 'Look after him,' and darted away up the stairs. Next moment they heard her saying, 'I'm here, Nonna. I had a bad dream so I went looking for you—I thought you were downstairs.'

'That's one thing she gets from her mother,' Drago said in a voice that shook slightly. 'She's never lost for words.'

'She's marvellous,' Alysa agreed.

'What did she say to you?'

'She told me to look after you, but I probably shouldn't have repeated that. Don't tell her.'

'I won't. Did she say why she thought I needed looking after?'

'She thinks Elena isn't nice to you.'

That deprived him of speech, she was interested to note. He simply ushered her outside and into the car. For some time he drove in silence, and she had the feeling that he was still disconcerted.

The city was quiet as they entered, and Alysa

realised that it was nearly one in the morning. In a few hours she seemed to have lived a whole lifetime, and time had lost all meaning.

'Is this the way to the hotel?' she asked after a while. 'Surely it's on the other side of the river?'

'I'm taking a slight detour, to show you something that may interest you. It's just along this road.'

At last he stopped the car outside an apartment block with an ornately decorated exterior, that looked several-hundred years old.

'This is where they lived,' he said when they were both standing on the pavement. 'Just up there.' He indicated one floor up.

It was a charming area, perfect for a love nest. Alysa studied it for a moment, then wandered down a short, narrow alley that ran along the side of the building and found herself overlooking the River Arno. A multitude of lights was on, their reflection gleaming in the water, and in the distance she could see the Ponte Vecchio, the great, beautiful bridge for which Florence was famous.

This was what James would have seen from the apartment window, standing with his lover in his arms. Here they had held each other, kissed, teased, spoken fond words, then taken each other to bed—while she had lain tormented in England, while the life of her baby had died out of her.

'That's their window,' Drago said. 'I once saw them standing there together.'

'You came to see them?'

'Yes, but I made sure they didn't find out. I skulked here like a lovesick schoolboy, hanging about to catch a glimpse of her, and retreating into the shadows when I saw her.' He paused and added wryly, 'And if you ever repeat that I'll deny it and sue you for every penny.'

'Don't worry, I did the same. I passed James's flat when I didn't need to. But I didn't see him. I suppose he'd already left.'

'You're lucky. I couldn't stay away from this place. I pictured them walking by the river, looking at the lights in the water, saying to each other the things that lovers have always said in this spot.'

'It's perfect for it,' she agreed, looking along the river to the Ponte Vecchio. 'It's the sort of place people mean when they say that Italy is a romantic country.'

The ironic way she said 'romantic' made him look at her in appreciation.

'It can be romantic,' he said. 'It can also be prosaic, businesslike and full of the most depressing common-sense. Romance doesn't lie in the country or the setting, but in the moment your eyes meet, and you know you're living in a world where there's only the two of you and nothing else exists.'

He added heavily, 'The night I saw them at that window, I knew they had found that world, and *I* no longer existed for her.'

Just then a brilliantly lit boat came along the river, casting its glow upward to where he stood leaning forward on the low wall, illuminating his harsh features. Regarding him dispassionately, Alysa realised that, though far from handsome, he had something that many women would have found attractive.

James had been wonderfully good-looking in a boyish, conventional way. But there was nothing boyish about Drago. He was a man—strong-willed, yielding nothing. His manners could be clumsy, and he lacked what was commonly called 'charm'.

Yet he had the mysterious something called 'presence'. In a room he would draw all eyes, not just because he was large, but because of his un-compromising air, and because he mattered.

And even Alysa, who had loved James pas-sionately, was fleetingly puzzled that Carlotta, the adored wife of Drago di Luca, had turned away from him and settled for less.

For herself men no longer existed. Otherwise she guessed she might have found him intriguing.

Drago was looking into the distance. Suddenly he dropped his head almost down to his chest, as though the burden had become too great to be borne.

She touched him. 'I know,' she whispered. 'I know.'

A cold wind was blowing from the river, and she shivered. Drago didn't speak, but he straight-ened up, putting his arms tightly around her, and rested his cheek on her head. It was the embrace of a comrade, not a lover, receiving her kindness thankfully, offering the same in return, and she accepted it, glad of the warmth.

'Are you all right?' he asked at last.

'I'm fine—fine. But I don't want to stay here any more.'

He kept his arm about her on the way back to

the car. On the journey back to the hotel she sat in silence, feeling hollowed out. When he drew up outside, he handed her a card.

'Here's how to contact me if you need to,' he said. 'I shall hope to see you tomorrow. If not— thank you for everything you've done for me.'

He leaned over and briefly kissed her cheek. *'Adio!'*

'Goodbye,' she said. 'I don't know if— Goodbye.'

She hurried into the hotel without looking back.

That night she dreamed of James as she hadn't done for months. The shield she'd created against him seemed to dissolve into mist, and he was there, standing at the window with Carlotta, laughing at her. She cried out for help, and for a moment seemed to sense Drago. But he vanished at once, and she knew herself to be alone again.

CHAPTER FOUR

IN THE morning she awoke unrefreshed, and the thought of going to the cemetery was suddenly more than she could bear. She would leave a day early, not risking another meeting with Drago.

But even as she thought this she was taking out clothes that might be proper for a ceremony in a graveyard. There was a severely tailored, dark-blue business suit complete with trousers. It occurred to her that she now owned very few skirts, and she'd brought none of them with her. Drago had been uncomfortably perceptive.

She donned the suit which was expensive, elegant and, above all, suitable.

This was something that had often made James tease her.

'Why does everything have to be so perfectly chosen, so *suitable*?' he'd demanded, half-fondly, half-exasperated. Strange that she'd never noticed that note in his voice until now.

'I'm a "suitable" person,' she'd teased back.

'Suitable for what?'

'Suitable for advising people on what to do with their money. I couldn't do that in a skimpy top and shorts. Hopefully I'll be suitable for a partnership in the firm.' She'd put her arms around him. 'But what I really want to be is suitable for you.'

'Ah, well, for that you need the skimpy top and shorts.'

Now, dressing to visit his grave, she tried not to remember that conversation, or the hectic hour in bed that had followed it.

She took a taxi there and arrived early, finding few other people, so that she had time to wander through the cemetery, studying the graves. Many of them were in family plots, carefully tended and adorned with flowers. One in particular held her attention because of the loving attention that had been lavished on it.

Everywhere that Alysa looked she saw red roses. They stretched up to the foot of the headstone with its ornate, carved decoration, and its two candle-holders, both with flickering candles that glowed against the picture of the woman buried beneath.

Looking closer, Alysa recognised Carlotta di Luca.

She stared. After everything that had happened the day before she'd thought nothing could surprise her again, but this lavish tribute went beyond what she had expected.

'*Ciao.*'

'*Sono Inglese,*' she said, turning to see a priest standing close by. He was elderly and had kindly eyes.

'Are you a friend of the family?' he asked.

'No,' she said quickly. 'I was just amazed to see roses at this time of year.'

'Her husband has an arrangement with a firm that imports flowers. This is an exceptional delivery for today, but there's a new bunch every week.'

Every week. After a whole year.

It might only have been for Tina, but she didn't believe it. They weren't just flowers, they were red roses, flaunted everywhere like a declaration. Drago was still passionately in love with the wife who had betrayed him.

'Do any of the others have roses?' she asked.

'Oh no, some of them are almost never visited, which is sad.'

'Just this one,' she mused.

'It's good to see a man so devoted to his wife. But I sense that he's still tormented by his memories, and has a long way to go before he finds peace.'

'Are all the victims buried here?'

'No. Some were visitors from other parts of the country, and their bodies were sent home— except for one, a man, who was a stranger. Nobody knew anything about him except his name and he was English. He didn't seem to have any family. He was buried over there.'

He indicated a far corner where several neat rows of small graves lay that were little more than slabs in the earth. The plot was neat and cared-for, but this was clearly the place for those with no relatives to pay for a fine headstone. Alysa wandered over slowly and went along the lines, seeking James. She found him at last at the very far end, near the corner.

'He looks so lonely out here,' she said.

'I know, this place is very sad. We tried to

contact his family in England, but he didn't seem to have one. I believe someone spoke to a young woman who was supposed to have known him well, but she sent back a message that he was nothing to do with her.'

'She shouldn't have done that,' Alysa murmured.

'Perhaps, but we'll never know what she might have been suffering. Ah, I see people arriving.'

She hardly noticed him moving away. She was looking at James's bare little plaque, tucked away in this lonely spot.

'Where I banished you,' she whispered.

It had never occurred to her before that James should be pitied, but now she saw him again at his best: young, laughing with the joy of life. She remembered how he'd broken into her austere existence, tempting her to enjoy new delights, teasing her. And his life had been snatched from him just when he had discovered his true joy. For the first time she knew sadness for his tragedy.

Now everyone was arriving for the ceremony, and Alysa stood back among the trees as Drago appeared. He seemed to be with a large family party that consisted not only of Tina and Elena, but several other adults and two children. Alysa watched until they had gone into the church, then she followed them quietly in and sat down at the back.

The family stayed close together. Tina's hand was in her father's, and on her other side a boy of about six was patting her shoulder. Glancing around the other families, she saw the same thing repeated in several different ways. These people were here to support each other in their loss. She was the only one isolated.

When the short service was over she slipped out of the door and went to stand among the trees once more. From here she could see the second part of the ceremony as the families walked among the graves and honoured their loved ones.

But for James there was nobody except herself.

'They've shunted you away so that you don't spoil their picture of the perfect wife and mother,' she told him sadly, looking down at the little slab that seemed so paltry on the ground. 'To everyone else but me, you don't exist.'

A step nearby made her turn to see Drago, looking drawn and tired.

'I sent the car to the hotel for you,' he said. 'You'd gone, but I still hoped to find you here.'

'I couldn't keep away. You knew that would happen, didn't you?'

He nodded.

'I guess you know me better than I know myself,' she said.

'Then it's the same for both of us,' he said quietly. 'Are you all right?'

'Yes, I'm fine. But you don't look as though you slept well.'

'I didn't sleep at all.'

'Was last night worse than you thought?'

'Not really. It was thinking about today that kept me awake. Carlotta's sister is here, with her husband and children.'

'And they don't know the truth either, so you have to do the performance for them too,' she said sympathetically.

'Exactly. But they'll be going tomorrow, so perhaps we could talk again?'

For a moment she hesitated. It would be good to enjoy the consolation of speaking freely, just once more. But it was a dangerous pleasure, one that she might come to enjoy too much.

Drago di Luca disturbed her. He was an impatient, domineering man, implacable in getting his own way, and if she'd met him under other circumstances she might have disliked him. But with her he was defenceless and it touched her heart.

But that was what made her wary. She'd worked so hard at deadening her heart, and now he threatened her peace.

'I don't know,' she said. 'It might not be a good idea.'

Drago glanced down at James's grave.

'Because of him?' he demanded. 'Why do you still bother with him?'

'Because he has nobody else.'

'And who do you have? Forget him and live your life. When Carlotta betrayed me, I did what had to be done and cut her out of my heart.'

'Hence the showers of red roses?'

'That's for Tina's sake. She needs to believe that I'm grieving.'

'You're deluding yourself. You're feeding your little girl nothing but pretty lies—'

'For her sake!'

'Is it? Is it only for her sake?'

He scowled, and she knew he had no answer. After a moment he said, 'What about you? Are you managing to cope?'

'Yes, I'm doing fine.'

'We need to talk again. I'll call you as soon as I can be rid of them.'

'No, Drago, it's better if we don't. We sorted out a lot of things last night, but there has to come a time when we say no more.'

A faint cry of, 'Poppa,' from behind made him look around.

'Just a moment,' he told Alysa. 'I'll be back. Don't go, please.'

He hurried off to talk to his daughter. After a brief hesitation Alysa began to back away under the trees. Her eyes were still fixed on him, noticing how, as soon as he joined the family, he seemed to become a different person—smiling, seemingly at ease, just as they expected.

She knew what it was doing to him inside, and part of her longed to respond to his plea for help. But now her sense of self-preservation was telling her to run for safety. When she'd backed away far enough, she turned and slipped out of the cemetery.

She spent the rest of the day strolling around Florence, looking at the sights without really seeing them. After all, it was only sensible to make the most of her brief trip. Then she blamed herself for prolonging the torment by trying to imagine James and Carlotta here in this lovely place, wandering the streets together, kissing in the shadows.

Then she admitted the truth: that she was avoiding Drago di Luca.

Everywhere looked the same, with no one place mattering more than another, no destination luring her.

'Nowhere to go,' she murmured wryly. 'That just about says it all.'

Darkness came early, bringing the lights on in the mediaeval streets. Almost of their own accord her steps turned to the Ponte Vecchio, the magnificent bridge over the River Arno that she had seen at a distance the night before. It was lined with shops on both sides, mostly jewellers and goldsmiths, and she strolled past them until she reached a shop at the end that sold not jewels but padlocks.

The window was full of them, covering shelves and hanging from the ceiling. The costliest jewels in the world couldn't have been displayed more lovingly. Looking closer, Alysa saw that many of them had tiny pictures etched on the side.

Just like the one she'd seen before, she thought. And there it was, nestling among the others—a padlock with a heart daintily engraved on it, so like the one James had given her and then secretly taken back that it might have been the same.

Alysa stared and blinked, as though hoping that she would see something else next time. But it was the same padlock.

'I don't understand,' she murmured.

She didn't know she'd spoken aloud, but a middle-aged man standing beside her grinned and spoke cheerily, first in Italian, then, when she looked puzzled, in English.

'You like my padlocks? They are the best in Florence.'

'I can see that,' she said politely. 'But why so many?'

'Why, for Cellini, of course.'

'I don't understand.'

'You've never heard of Benvenuto Cellini?'

'I know he was a great Florentine goldsmith and sculptor in the sixteenth century, but that's all.'

'Come and meet him.'

Taking her arm gently, the man led her to the end of the bridge, where she found a bust of

Cellini raised high on an ornate plinth. It was impressive and elegant, but what caught Alysa's attention were the railings that surrounded it, which were covered with padlocks. Hundreds of them.

'Lovers put them there,' the shop owner confided. 'It's an old tradition. They buy a padlock, lock it onto the railings and throw the key into the River Arno. That means that their love has locked them together for all time, even unto death.'

'How—how beautiful,' Alysa stammered. A terrible dread was rising in her.

'Isn't it charming? It's also good business, because when lovers come to me I usually manage to sell them three. Then they leave one with Cellini, and each gives one to the other, but they also swap keys so that only they can open each other's locks.'

'Can I see some of them?' she asked, speaking in a daze.

'Of course. It's this way back to the shop.'

Once there he spread a collection on the counter, and she picked up the one that was exactly like James's gift, the heart studded with tiny stones.

'Ah, yes, everyone likes that,' the shopkeeper

said. 'They're real diamonds and it's the most expensive one I have.'

'Even unto death,' she murmured.

'That's the part that always affects them,' he said. 'They know they'll be together for eternity.'

There in her mind was the picture of James and Carlotta, lying in the smashed chair, dead in the same moment. Together for eternity.

'How much?' she asked in a bleak voice.

He told her the price and she gasped.

'Yes, you'd have to be really in love to pay so much,' he conceded. He lowered his voice conspiratorially. 'If your lover gives you this one, then you can rely on him for ever.'

'Oh yes,' she murmured. 'For ever.'

'Why don't you bring him in to see it?'

'I think we're a bit past that point,' she said wryly. 'Thank you, but I must be going.'

She fled while she still had some self-command, turning back across the bridge so that she didn't have to pass the statue again with its terrible display of lovers' vows.

James and Carlotta had been here, hung a padlock on the railings, tossed the key into the Arno and swore love unto death. Then they had exchanged padlocks, each taking the other's key. That was what she'd found in his bag, and that was why the key hadn't fitted. It was all so clear when you knew.

She'd told herself that nothing could hurt her any more, but she found she was shaking as she'd done so often in the past. But, instead of weeping, she began to laugh at this last deadly joke that had lain in wait for her. It was hilarious, the funniest thing that had ever happened.

She made her way blindly along the streets, shuddering, laughing, pressing her hand to her mouth, knowing that she was receiving strange looks, caring nothing for them, or even for the fact that she was lost.

Now she was in a quiet part of the city, within sight of the river, and went down to lean on a low wall overlooking the water. Vaguely, downstream, she thought she could see the apartment building where Drago had taken her last night—the place where James and Carlotta had been free to indulge their love.

And, to her dismay, she was swept with longing for the one person in the world who she could reach out to at this moment. If Drago were here she would run to him, blurt out her misery, knowing that he would understand everything that was too hard for her to say. And she would find his powerful arms open to her in comfort. She had no doubt of it.

He'd known that soon her brave façade would collapse, leaving her defenceless. He alone had seen the fear behind the mask, because it was so like his own.

The need for him was so strong that she took out her mobile phone and found the card with his number. But when she'd dialled two figures she stopped and hurriedly turned the phone off.

'What am I doing?' she whispered. 'I must be mad. Everything that happened last night just wasn't real. I've got to get home to England, then everything will be normal again.'

Using the river as a guide, she finally managed to make her way back to the hotel.

'There are some messages for you,' the young man at the desk told her, pushing a paper towards her. 'The gentleman sounded urgent.'

'Thank you. Please have my bill ready first thing tomorrow. I want to leave early. And, if anyone else should call, please tell them I haven't returned.'

She was booked on the two o'clock flight the next day; she would leave for the airport as early as possible. In her room she packed hurriedly, ignoring the phone when it began to ring.

She was afraid he would turn up at her hotel, but to her relief he didn't. At last the phone stopped ringing, and she gave muttered thanks that Drago had given up.

Next morning she left quickly. Luck was with her. There was an earlier flight with vacant seats and she managed to change her ticket. After checking in, she went to wait in the departure lounge, telling herself that soon she would be free. Just a little longer…

'Excuse me, *signorina*.'

She looked up to find a man in uniform.

'Signorina Dennis?'

'Yes.'

'Will you come with me, please?'

'But I'm about to board the plane.'

'I'm afraid you can't do so until we have cleared up a small matter.'

His manner was pleasant but firm, and she yielded reluctantly.

'This way to my office,' he said.

She followed him, impatient to hear his explanation, but when they reached his office he showed her in and retreated, closing the door, leaving Alysa alone with the man who was waiting there.

'*You!*' she said angrily. 'I might have known!'

Drago didn't reply immediately, and she had time to study him. Now she wondered how she'd recognised him. If his face had been haggard the day before, it was deathly now. A man who'd seen a ghastly vision might have had his burning eyes. But she refused to feel sympathy. She couldn't afford it.

'I'm sorry,' he said at last. 'I would much rather not have had to do this, but something has happened. You can't go back to England until you know everything.'

'There you go again, telling me what I can and can't do. Who do you think you are?'

'I'm the only person in the world who can fill the gaps in your knowledge, just as you did for me—except that there's much more than either of us dreamed.'

'I don't want to know. You must be mad to— Actually getting someone to fetch me from the departure lounge—how did you do that?'

'Pietro, the young man who brought you here, owes me a favour.'

'And what about my luggage? It's on the plane.'

'It'll be retrieved.'

'It must be a very big favour,' she said bitingly.

'I wouldn't have done it if I hadn't been at my wits' end. You ignored my messages, and when I went to your hotel this morning they said you'd left early. But I checked your flight and it was two o'clock. I thought I'd find you easily, but I discovered that you'd changed to the earlier flight. I had to do something.'

'And everyone had to simply step aside,' she seethed. 'But not me. I'm going back to get on the plane, and don't you dare to stop me. Get out of my way!'

Drago had positioned himself between her and the door, and showed no sign of moving.

'You're not leaving,' he said quietly. 'You're coming with me.'

'So now I'm a prisoner?'

'If you like to put it that way. I'm sorry. I don't like behaving like this, but I have no choice. Alysa, for pity's sake, won't you try to understand?'

'I understand that everyone has to do what you

want because you don't recognise the word no. Enough! I'm not a pawn for you to move around, and I'm leaving right now.'

'This is important!'

'I don't care what it is. I'm finished. Now, for the last time, *get out of my way!*'

He didn't budge. If anything he seemed to dig himself in further, and Alysa prepared for battle. If he thought he could make her yield again, he would learn that he was mistaken.

But then something happened that caught her off-balance. Suddenly his shoulders sagged, as if a vital link had snapped inside him. Without further argument he pulled open the door and spoke heavily.

'Pietro, please escort the *signorina* back to the departure lounge.'

He moved out of Alysa's path, and she hurried to the door.

'Thank you,' she said. 'I'm sorry to disappoint you, but I really have to go.'

She could have got away then but she made the mistake of turning back and seeing something she would much rather not have seen. Drago looked defeated, as if he'd simply abandoned all hope.

'Please try to understand,' she begged.

'I do understand. You'd better go quickly.'

But instead of leaving she made her next mistake: going to look him in the eye, and saying, 'I don't want you to think— Look at me.' She put a hand on his arm and he raised his head to meet her gaze. His aggression had died, leaving only weariness behind. 'You're not being fair,' she protested desperately. 'You must realise that I can't—'

'I know,' he agreed. 'I shouldn't have done it this way. I was desperate, but you're right, it's not really your problem. You've done all you could, and I'm grateful.'

'And now I have to return to whatever I can make of my life, because I can't— *Oh, all right!*' The last words were almost a shout of exasperation.

'All right? What does that mean?'

'It means I give in. You've won. The new tactic worked. I'll come with you.'

The joy on his face was a startling revelation. The next moment she was engulfed in a bear hug. Somehow she found herself returning it, even laughing with him, because the violence of his relief was infectious.

'Just let me breathe,' she gasped.

He drew back to look at her. 'Thank you,' he said fervently.

'Just don't ever do this to me again.'

'When this is over, I swear you'll never have to see me. Let's go.'

'Yes, let's, before I change my mind. What about my bags? They'll be on the plane by now.'

'Pietro will get them off, and he knows where to send them. Come on.'

CHAPTER FIVE

OUTSIDE he showed her to his car—not the one he'd driven before, but far larger and more powerful. He swung confidently out of the airport onto the main road and drove fast for a few miles before swinging off.

'Where are you going?' she asked. 'This isn't the way to Florence.'

'We're not going to Florence, we're going to another little place I own, in the mountains. We need privacy.'

'What about Tina?'

'She and Elena are spending a few days with her aunt and uncle. You saw them at the cemetery.'

'So if they're gone why can't we have privacy in your house in Florence?'

'Because I have curious employees. I want total isolation, and we'll only get that in the mountains.'

Total isolation with this man, cut off from help if things went wrong. The thought should have made her nervous, but it didn't. She'd already been through the worst. Now they were like two comrades facing enemy fire together. To be comrades you only needed trust. And, despite his outrageous behaviour, she did trust him.

The land began to slope gently upwards; the buildings became further apart. Sometimes the road wound its way among tall trees for miles, so that it felt as though they were the only two people in the world. Despite the time of year the weather was bright, and the sun glittered through the branches, dappling the way ahead.

Suddenly there was a gap in the trees, revealing the land sloping away. Alysa watched, fascinated, as they climbed higher and higher, seeming to leave the ground behind, soaring into a different world.

At last the road levelled out and they were driving through a small village. Drago stopped the car.

'I'm just going to buy a few things,' he said. 'Will you come with me, or wait here?'

'I'll come with you.'

At any other time she would have found the

village fascinating, coming, as it seemed to, from another age. Some streets were cobbled; the buildings were large and decorative, with archways extending out over the pavement. Impossible to imagine a supermarket here. Drago went from shop to shop, buying fresh meat and vegetables with the confidence of an expert. Every shopkeeper knew him.

'Haven't seen you here for a while, *signore*,' one observed. 'Nice to have you back. I've got something in stock that I think you'll like.'

Then there was bread, cheese, milk and oil to be bought. Again the counter assistants greeted him as an old friend and produced his favourite items at once.

'Don't worry, I'm a good cook,' he told Alysa.

'Yes, I was really worried about that,' she said dryly.

He gave her a look of appreciation for this sally, and handed her a couple of bags to carry. Since he was weighed down by even more bags himself, she couldn't even protest.

She told herself that she'd been kidnapped, and it was an outrage, but it felt more like going on a picnic. There was only one thing to do, and that was to stop fighting it and go with the flow.

'What's the matter?' Drago asked her.

'Matter?'

'You were staring into the distance.'

'Nothing's the matter,' she said robustly. 'Come on. Let's get going.'

Then they were on the road again, climbing among the trees, until he turned suddenly, and in a few moments they were drawing up before a small villa. There were no lights on and the place looked glum and chilly. She shivered as he unlocked the door.

'It'll be better when I've lit the range,' he said. 'It starts the central heating.'

'You have to do that by hand?'

'This is the mountains,' he said by way of explanation. 'It's different up here. Why don't you unpack the food in the kitchen—but don't touch anything apart from that.'

'I should be used to you ordering me about by now,' she observed.

'Yes, you should.'

He got to work on the range in the kitchen, piling logs in until the flames flickered up between them, then tossing charcoal on top. When two dials on the pipes showed the same high temperature, he switched on the central heating, and the place began to warm up quickly.

She began to wander around, somewhat surprised by the cosy informality of the place, which had none of the studied luxury to be found in the Florence villa. Here there were wooden floors with rugs tossed about, apparently casually. The furniture was old, even slightly shabby, and the place had a friendly atmosphere that appealed to her.

The villa was built on a steep slope, with the garage at the bottom. Next to it was a woodshed, and the rest of the place was built on top, so that, looking out of the window, she found she was on a level with the branches of the trees. The light was beginning to fade, so that she could see only shadows below, and the effect was like floating away from the earth.

'This is yours,' Drago said, opening a door and showing her into a room dominated by a large bed.

'How long are you planning for me to stay?' she asked.

'I think we'll be here tomorrow, and perhaps leave the day after. It depends on a lot of things.'

'Why don't you tell me why I'm here?'

'Let's eat first. Your bags should arrive soon.'

When he'd gone she took out her mobile phone and called her office. She'd booked herself a week off, but had hinted that she would return earlier—which had won the approval of her boss, Brian Hawk, who had always helped and encouraged her. Now she told him that she would take the full week.

'I wish you'd given me a bit more warning,' he grumbled. 'There's a lot happening at the moment.'

'I've been detained by something unexpected,' she said truthfully.

'Well, I hope you sort it out soon. Your prospects are bright, Alysa. Don't spoil them by being unreliable.'

When she'd hung up she sat considering these last words, wondering why she wasn't filled with alarm. Her dream was to be offered a partnership, and for this she'd worked hard and sometimes brilliantly, earning Brian's praise. In the last year she'd redoubled her efforts, staying in the office late to avoid returning to her empty apartment, and then taking work home with her.

Once Brian's warning would have alerted her to danger, but now the words seemed to come from a distance. It was true, of course. She would have to be careful. But she could think about it later.

Looking at the double bed, she wondered if this was the room where Drago and Carlotta had slept together. A glance into the wardrobe confirmed it. Some of Carlotta's clothes were still here, suggesting that she'd abandoned them when she'd begun her new life, and Drago couldn't bring himself to dispose of them.

When she emerged a few minutes later he was already at work in the kitchen, doing something mysterious with oil and vegetables.

'The one thing I never thought of you doing was cooking,' she mused, studying him.

'We're not like the English, who think cooking's sissy unless you're a celebrity chef earning a fortune. My mother thought a man wasn't a real man unless he could cook.'

'What are you making?'

'*Pappa al pomadoro*—bread cooked with garlic, parsley, basil, salt, oil and tomatoes.'

'I'm impressed. And afterwards?'

'Just be patient.'

He was immersed in what he was doing, and seemed to have forgotten the reason he'd brought her here, although he'd claimed it was important. With another man she might have suspected a trick to lure her into a seduction, but not with Drago. He was in the grip of a purpose so inflexible that he could afford to set it aside until the right moment.

'Can I do anything to help?' she asked.

'Yes, you could watch this saucepan while I light the fire in the other room.'

'A fire as well as central heating?'

'Wait till you see it.'

A few minutes later she understood. The fire, nestled in a neat grate, was small but delightful, throwing darting lights over the room. While it offered little heat, it created an atmosphere of warmth and comfort that no central heating could match.

'My mother always lit a fire in the evenings,' Drago said. 'When I looked this place over the agent said it could all be renovated and the fireplace taken out. I told him to forget it. I wanted everything left just as it was.'

'Is this the place you told me about, where you and Carlotta came when you married?'

'Yes, it is. After she died I wanted to sell it, but Tina loves it, so I couldn't. Perhaps I shouldn't have brought you up here, but I couldn't think of anywhere else where we'd have some privacy.'

'It's all right. Is there anything more I can do?'

'You could lay the table. You'll find everything over there, including wine glasses.'

He indicated an old-fashioned dresser and she got to work, finding a table cloth and cutlery. In a few minutes Drago emerged from the kitchen to serve the first course and open a bottle of white wine.

She suddenly realised that she was ravenous. She'd left the hotel too quickly to eat very much, and had managed only a sandwich at the airport. The *pappa al pomadoro* had a delicious smell that drove everything else out of her head, and the taste was every bit as good.

'I needed this,' she said with a sigh.

'After the day I've given you, you mean?'

'Well, I admit you're making up for it.'

'One thing I've been wanting to ask you—when

you agreed to come with me, you said, "the new tactic worked". What did you mean by that?'

'You know very well what I meant by that,' she said indignantly. 'When giving me orders didn't work, you backed off and played the reasonable card.'

'Is that what I did?'

'Didn't you?'

He hesitated. 'It wasn't all calculated. I could see I was doing everything wrong, driving you away. I tend to approach things with hobnailed boots, I know that. And when it doesn't work...' He made a helpless gesture. 'I sometimes don't know what to do next. And just then—I felt like such a loser. I didn't have the heart to fight any more.'

'You?' she asked with a hint of teasing. 'Stop fighting?'

He gave her a wry look. 'I guess I deserved that. It's almost funny that you accused me of playing the "reasonable card". I'm not good at being reasonable. Ask anyone who knows me.'

'I don't need to. I'm beginning to know you myself.'

'That's an unnerving thought.'

'Why? You don't try to hide it. Everything's upfront. Can I have some more of this?'

'Just a little. You've got to leave room for the steak.'

The steak was delicious, followed by a loaf made of flour, sugar, eggs and butter. With each course he changed the wine.

'I won't ask why you vanished so suddenly yesterday,' Drago said. 'I guess I asked for it. But I tried to call you for the rest of the day, and you'd switched your phone off. I wondered if you'd gone back to the waterfall so that you could see it without a crowd.'

'No, I just went walking around Florence.'

The constraint in her voice made him look at her quickly and ask, 'Did you go back to their apartment?'

'No, why should you think that?'

'Because something happened yesterday that hurt you more than you have been already.'

'Well, yes.'

'Can't you tell me?' he asked when she fell silent.

'You remember I said that when James came back from Florence in September he was a bit strange?' Drago nodded. 'But I didn't mention the padlock I found in his things. Yesterday I found out about Benvenuto Cellini.'

'You mean the statue at the end of the Ponte Vecchio?'

'And the padlocks.'

'Did he and Carlotta exchange them?'

'They must have done. He said the one I found was for me. But after we broke up I came home one day and he'd been there while I was out, fetching some personal stuff he'd left behind. The padlock was missing too. He must have gone through my things. He didn't leave a note or anything, just his key on the table.'

'I'm beginning to get a picture of this man,' Drago said slowly. 'He liked to do things in a way that was easiest on himself—going to your home when you weren't there.' His mouth twisted in contempt. 'And this is the man my Carlotta preferred.'

'I guess she hadn't discovered that side of him yet,' Alysa reflected. 'He just didn't like confrontation.'

'I wonder how he and Carlotta would have managed after a while,' Drago mused, looking into his wine glass.

'Did she like confrontation?'

'She was never backward about telling people what she thought.'

'Just like you. The two of you must have had some terrific fights.'

'Spectacular,' he confirmed. 'She once said— she once said she loved me because I was the only man she knew who could stand up to her. She'd have got bored with James in time.'

'And you'd have taken her back for Tina's sake?'

'Yes. What about you?'

'No,' she said slowly. 'I didn't know before, but I know now. I would never have taken James back in a million years.'

'Let's drink our coffee and brandy by the fire,' Drago said.

They cleared the plates into the kitchen, but he rejected her offer to wash up, steering her firmly back into the living room and towards an armchair close to the fire on one side. Another one stood on the other side, and he threw himself into this.

'That was the best meal I've ever tasted,' Alysa said sincerely.

'Thank you. I guess I owed you a decent meal.'

'I think you needed it too. You look more relaxed.'

'Cooking does that for me,' he admitted. 'Going to the cemetery with the whole family was very tough, having to watch every word in case they guessed. You can't imagine how I longed for the one person I can be honest with.' He raised his brandy glass to her.

'Yes, I can,' she murmured. 'Me too.'

He was about to answer when his mobile phone sounded. He answered and immediately his face became exasperated and horrified.

'I told Pietro to send them up here,' he barked. 'What does he think he—? How soon can you get them here? Why not tonight? All right, but first thing tomorrow.'

'Shall I guess?' Alysa asked as he hung up. 'My bags?'

'Pietro took them to the villa. I thought I made myself plain, but evidently I didn't. I'm sorry. That was my steward wanting to know what he should do. You find it funny?'

Alysa had given a little laugh. Now she said lightly, 'It does have its funny side. You were so determined to avoid the curious eyes of your employees.'

'I apologise for all this,' he growled. 'They can't get out here tonight, not in the dark on that mountain road. Your things will be here tomorrow, but until then—'

'I'll cope.'

'Alysa, I swear I didn't plan this.'

'It's all right, I believe you,' she said through laughter. 'With another man I'd be suspicious, but you and I aren't about that.'

'Thank you.'

She had set her brandy glass down on a small fender before the fire. Now she reached forward to get it, and kept on sliding down until she was sitting on the floor, finding it surprisingly comfortable because of the thick rug that seemed to be made of fake fur. She leaned back against the chair, sipping contentedly.

She was enveloped by a sense of well-being. It had something to do with the fire and the fine brandy, but more to do with Drago. He'd said, 'the one person I can be honest with', and it was true for her too.

She thought of the journey home that she'd nearly taken: landing at the airport with nobody to meet her, queuing for a taxi, reaching her home to find it cold, dark and empty, as it had been for the past endless year. The lonely evening with only her bleak thoughts for company.

Here she was effectively a prisoner, but a well-fed prisoner, basking in the glow of a friendly fire, relaxed and almost happy. If she could have escaped she would not have done so. She sighed pleasurably, feeling her cares fade away.

Drago, happening to glance across at her, saw the brandy glass about to slip out of her hand and hastened to remove it. Her eyes were closed, and her breathing coming steadily.

He studied her, feeling guilty but unable to stop. It was unforgivable to watch her while she was unaware, but something about her face held him against his will. Now that her defences were abandoned, she'd changed in a way that made him grow still.

If asked to describe her mouth he would have said that it was too firm and precise to be attractive, but exactly right for the slightly grim female she'd been at their first meeting. No man, he thought, considering the matter impartially, would ever be tempted to kiss that mouth.

But now it was softened, her lips slightly apart, the breath whispering through them. Nature had shaped her more generously than she wanted the world to know, and sleep had revealed what she had tried to hide.

Her whole face was one that a man might contemplate with curiosity, even while he blamed himself for his impertinence.

She stirred and he backed off, rising to his feet and going to a chest of drawers where he'd deposited a canvas bag when he'd first come in. Having retrieved it he returned to his seat. For a while he remained still, until at last, with evident reluctance, he reached inside, drew out an envelope and sat turning it over between his fingers. He did this for some time, making no attempt to open it, and putting it aside quickly when Alysa stirred and yawned.

'Have I been asleep?' she demanded.

'Just dozing for a minute.'

'How rude of me. I'm sorry.' She pulled herself up and rubbed her eyes, gazing into the fire which cast a glow over her face.

'Well?' she said at last, turning to look at him.

'Well?'

'Well, why are we here? Drago, when are you going to stop putting things off? You wanted to show me something so important that you dragooned me into coming here, but then you seemed to forget all about it.'

'I've been trying not to think of it,' he admitted. 'It's something that was found in their apartment and only delivered to my house yesterday.'

'But didn't you go through the place?'

'Yes, and I thought I'd been pretty thorough, but it seems there was a secret place—a small cupboard in the wall that you'd never find unless you knew it was there. The people who rent the place now discovered it by accident and found a box inside, containing a cache of letters. From them they learned enough to get in touch with me.'

'You mean…?'

'Letters between James and Carlotta, dating from September, as soon as he went back to England after their first meeting. When he came to live here he brought her letters with him. His were sent to her work, and I suppose that's where she kept them, because I had no idea.'

She had to force herself to ask, 'What do they say?'

'I haven't read them.'

'How could you bear not to?'

He smiled faintly. 'Because you weren't there. I've always thought of myself as a brave man, but I found I can't do this alone.' His smile became self-mocking. 'I need you to hold my hand.'

'If you haven't read them, how can you be sure they're real? James wasn't a man for writing letters. He did it all by phone and email, like most people these days.'

He showed her the envelope. 'There are some things that you can't trust to email. Is this his handwriting?'

'Yes,' she said slowly, taking it from him. 'That's James.'

She pulled out the letter and looked at the date.

'September,' she murmured. 'He must have written this as soon as he came back.'

The words seemed to leap off the page.

I'm sitting here at midnight, trying to imagine that I'm still there with you. It's only a few hours since you kissed me goodbye at the airport, yet already it seems like a life-time. All I can do is try to tell you what our meeting has meant to me, how you've transformed my life in only a few days.

She laid down the letter. 'I can't read any more.'
But even as she said it she began reading again. James had written these words on the night he'd returned from Florence in September. She'd met him at the airport, gone home with him, tried to make love to him and been rejected.

'Because he'd come from her bed only a few hours before,' she whispered. 'He sent me away, then sat down to write to her.'

Drago was reaching into the bag, pulling out more letters, searching through them feverishly.

'What does she say to him?' Alysa asked.

'She says here that her marriage is a sham,' Drago replied in a dazed voice. 'And she can endure it no longer. *Mio dio!*'

Alysa barely heard. She too was pulling out letters, seeking the ones from James. They were revealing. He wrote:

My darling, please don't be jealous of Alysa. She means nothing to me any more.

Even at its best it was only an insipid love, nothing compared to what I feel for you.

And in another letter:

I've promised to be with you next week, and I will. Don't worry about my failing you, because I never will. I've made an excuse to Alysa and she's accepted it. Luckily she'll believe anything I tell her.

So I'll arrive on that plane, and, if you can be there to meet me, wonderful. If not, I'll just go to our little home and wait for you.

'It's true,' she said. 'I believed whatever he told me, I loved him so much.'

In answer to Drago's look she handed him the letter.

'It's dated just before my birthday,' she said. 'We had such plans. But then he said he had to go away for a few days—something to do with the prospect of a job as a photographer. When he came back he said he hadn't got the job and it had been a wasted few days.'

'You didn't check up on him?'

'I never checked up on him. I trusted him totally. I didn't know he despised me for it.'

'And now you can despise him,' Drago said fiercely. 'Let that be your revenge.'

'Yes,' she said in what she hoped was a strong voice. 'You're right, of course.'

But the words echoed bleakly through the emptiness inside her.

CHAPTER SIX

DRAGO studied the contents of the next letter with a set face that grew almost cruel as he read on.

You say your husband is a harsh man. My love, it breaks my heart to think of you trapped there with him, the victim of his bullying. But it won't be long now before I come to rescue you.

'It's a lie!' Drago said violently. 'I never bullied her. Others maybe, but not her or Tina, I swear it.'

'You don't need to convince me,' Alysa said.

'But how could she tell such a lie?' he demanded.

'She was playing a part, saying what she thought would fire him up.'

She took the letter from him and scanned it quickly, finding it full of a tender possessiveness that she would have thought charming in any other man. James was writing to the woman he had passionately adored, and it was so different from the casual love he'd given her that her heart ached.

Or at least it would have ached, if she hadn't been safely past that stage, she reassured herself.

There was more about Drago, making it clear that Carlotta had painted him in a tyrannical light. Alysa found herself disbelieving every word. Already she knew him well enough for that. It was he who was Carlotta's victim, raging helplessly like a baited bear.

'We were together for ten years,' he grated. 'Until she left me, I thought they were wonderful years. We loved and cared for each other.'

'And you were always faithful to her, weren't you?' It was a statement, not a question.

'Of course I was faithful,' he said scornfully. 'I was hers in every way, body and soul. There's nothing I wouldn't have done for her. *Nothing!*'

The last word was a shout of anguish. Alysa moved instinctively, taking his hand between both of hers. He gripped her so hard that she winced, but concealed it, letting him hold onto her as long as he needed.

'Sorry,' he said ruefully as he released her. 'Did I hurt you?'

'Not at all,' she lied, flexing her fingers.

'Do you want to stop?'

'No, we can't give in now. We've got to follow the path wherever it leads. After all, we already know the worst.'

She began to read aloud.

'"Talking to you last night was wonderful, but I wish it hadn't had to be the telephone. I so much wanted to tell you our wonderful secret in person, and see your dear face".'

'What secret?' Drago asked. 'Does she say?'

Alysa didn't reply. A suffocating fear was overtaking her. It was impossible. She was mad even to think of it. She told herself she must read on, and then, '"It's the most wonderful thing in the world. I thought nothing could make our love more perfect, but our baby will make us complete".'

'Baby!' Drago sat up, tense.

In a daze, Alysa read on. '"My darling, never doubt that this child is yours. Since the day I met you I've kept my husband out of my bed, and no man but you has loved me. No man ever will again".'

'*Bastardo!*' Drago snatched the letter out of her hand and began to read it urgently. After a moment he crumpled it in his hand.

'I don't believe this,' he muttered. 'Why does she say things that can't be true?'

'Can't they?' Alysa asked, watching the fire intently. 'Did she "keep you out", as she says?'

'Yes, but—' He broke off with a groan. 'A few months earlier I'd told her I wanted another child, but she put me off. We quarrelled and she shut me out. I wanted to be reconciled, but she wouldn't— Now I see that it was more convenient to keep me away, because all the time—'

He slammed his hand down on a low table with such force that it smashed. A stream of violent Italian curses broke from him. His chest was heaving with the violence of his emotion, and for a moment he was too distracted to watch Alysa—and so didn't see that she was staring into space, her face wooden, her eyes dead.

She and Carlotta had become pregnant by James at almost exactly the same time. When she'd been waiting for him to arrive for Christmas, thinking how she would tell him of their baby, he had been on his way to Florence—to Carlotta, and the child he'd fathered with her.

Half unconsciously she laid her hand over her stomach, almost deafened by the thunderous beat of her own heart.

She'd thought there could be no more pain beyond what she had already suffered. She was wrong.

She climbed slowly to her feet and moved away from the fire's warmth to the window, where she stared out, unseeing. After a moment Drago came and stood beside her.

'I'm glad you couldn't understand what I was saying,' he said. 'I thought I was ready for anything, but that one—after all this time. I don't know what I want to do—throw something, bang my head against the wall, curse her to hell and back.'

But she astonished him by shrugging.

'Why bother? We knew they were sleeping together. This doesn't really make any difference.'

Drago stared, alerted less by her words than by a note in her voice that he'd heard before: harsh. Dead. It was how she'd sounded when they had first met at the waterfall, and it had fitted with the robotic severity of her appearance that day. Today that chilling note had briefly gone, revealing a vibrant sound that had suggested a whole new side to her, but now it was back like steel armour.

He'd criticised her for it then, but not now. He was beginning to understand.

'Does it really not make a difference?' he asked carefully.

'Why should it?' She gave a brittle laugh. 'What's one more betrayal? They've been dead a year. Good riddance!'

She leaned back against the window frame and regarded him with cool detachment as she observed, 'I told you there was a lot to be said for putting it behind you, and now you see I was right.'

'Then I envy you,' he said untruthfully.

He could hardly speak for horror at what he was witnessing. She was turning to stone before his eyes, retreating into a place where he couldn't follow. If he tried she would fight him off with deadly weapons. A sensible man would have feared her, but he could only feel a surge of pity, followed by anger at himself. What had he done to her?

His attention was caught by something floating past the window. Throwing it open, he saw a blanket of white. Thick flakes of snow poured down onto the leaves, through the branches and down to the ground far below. While they'd been unaware, the world had changed beyond recognition.

'It looks so cold out there,' Alysa whispered. 'So cold.' She turned away. 'I think I'll go to bed now.'

He wished she would meet his eyes. Her withdrawn look unsettled him.

'Are you all right?' he asked, feeling how inadequate the question was.

'Of course. I'm just tired.'

'This snow will block the roads, and delay your bags getting here. You'll find some clothes in the wardrobe, but I'm afraid they're hers.'

'Don't worry about me,' she said indifferently. 'I don't need—' she shuddered '—anything of hers. There's no need to show me the way. Goodnight.'

She walked away to the bedroom, moving carefully because she was afraid that any moment she would break in two. When she was inside she leaned back against the door and stayed there for several minutes, trying to find the strength to move.

Her mind was focussed. *Keep calm. Stay in control. Don't go mad. Above all, cling onto your sanity.*

'It doesn't really change anything,' she muttered. 'What difference can it make now?'

But even as the words came she wrapped her arms around herself and bent double, as if to protect the child who was already lost. Still doubled up, she managed to get to the bed, where she breathed deeply until she felt her strength return a little.

'Unpack,' she said as though it was only by giving herself instructions that she could function. 'I've got to make sure it's there.'

'It' was a small bag containing underwear and make-up that she always carried in her hand luggage ever since an airline had lost her bags for three days. She found it quickly, much to her relief, as no power on earth would have made her wear Carlotta's clothes.

But curiosity made her pull open drawers to

see what was there. Carlotta hadn't got round to clearing out this place, and there were still traces of her in lacy bras and panties, delicately made and shaped to be sexy rather than functional. There were nightdresses too, frothy and transparent, cut low.

How could any woman bear to leave such beautiful things behind? Because she was buying a new wardrobe for a new lover, of course. Alysa regarded them with cold contempt.

She thought of Carlotta's photographs, which had emphasised intelligence over beauty, but these items told another story. This was a woman totally at ease with her own sexuality, happy to emphasise it—flaunt it, even—with more than one man.

She had shared this place with her husband, entrancing him with garments so sparely cut that they were almost non-existent. Then she had gone to James and worked her magic on him until she, Alysa, had vanished from his mind.

'It doesn't matter,' she said, repeating the mantra that sustained her. 'Nothing that happens now makes any difference.'

But the mantra was becoming meaningless. The more she tried to hold it up as a shield, the more useless it became. The strength that had kept her controlled for a year was vanishing fast so that the grief came welling up inside.

'No,' she said hoarsely. 'No, *no!* I won't let it—'

She couldn't have said what she meant. Her hands were moving independently of her mind, pulling open drawers, tossing the contents out onto the bed, the floor, reaching into the bag for scissors. She didn't know that tears were streaming down her face as she made the first slash and saw a filmy nightdress disintegrate.

Another slash, another, and now she was no longer destroying clothes but plunging a knife into the heart of the woman who'd stolen her love, killed her child and turned her life into a desert. She'd longed to do this for a year. She knew that now.

She stopped only when her strength had drained away. Sitting on the bed, she surveyed the devastation around her. None of Carlotta's clothes were intact; some had been ripped to tiny shreds. Shocked, she stared at them while her body heaved, as the dam broke and the sobs that had been repressed too long forced their way to the surface.

The scream that broke from her might have come from someone else. It went on and on, louder, more shrill, full of an agony that would never end.

The next moment the door burst open and Drago stood there.

'Alysa, what—?' He stopped as he took in the sight of the devastated room, then froze as he saw the scissors still in her hand.

Following his gaze, Alysa tossed the scissors into a corner and stood facing him, breathing heavily.

'For pity's sake, what's the matter?' he breathed. 'Come here.'

'Don't touch me!' she screamed. *'Don't touch me!'*

He reached for her but she eluded him, dodging past him, out and down the stairs to the front door.

'Alysa!' he cried vainly, trying to catch up. 'Don't go out into the snow. You'll catch your death.'

But she was gone. Drago raced down the stairs and out of the front door to find himself confronting a blizzard. The snow had whipped up to a storm into which she had vanished without trace.

'Alysa!' Drago shouted. 'Come back. It's dangerous out there.'

But she was gone in the whirling wall of flakes. Appalled, Drago realised that she could have taken any direction, have slipped on the steep slope, perhaps broken her neck.

'Alysa!' he cried again, but the only reply was the scream of the wind.

He began to stumble after her, but, without knowing which way she'd turned, he was lost. He doubled back, calling her name fruitlessly, becoming more alarmed by the minute.

He lost track of time. It might have been five minutes before the wind died, or it might have been hours, but at last the noise was replaced by an eerie silence. He called again and again, hoping to hear her call back, but all that returned was the echo.

He tried not to think of the worst that could have happened to her. Then a sound from nearby made him turn sharply, but he couldn't see her. He listened and heard it again; it was coming from the ground, like an animal whimpering in pain. He began to move around cautiously until he nearly fell over a mound at the foot of a tree. It was covered in snow and it took him a moment to realise that this was Alysa.

'*Mio dio!*' He dropped to his knees, urgently brushing snow away from her. 'What are you doing?'

She didn't seem to hear, but lay with her eyes closed, shaking violently and uttering a long, agonised moan. He said her name again and again, shaking her gently. When she didn't respond he pulled her to her feet.

'Come on,' he said, lifting her in his arms. 'The sooner I get you into the warm, the better.'

Moving as fast as he could he made it back to the villa and ran upstairs to the bathroom. To his relief her eyes were open, and she seemed a little more aware of her surroundings.

'Take off those wet clothes and get under a hot shower,' he said.

He hung a towelling robe on the door and got out, hurrying back to her room. The sight of it covered in ripped-up clothes shocked him anew, but he got to work quickly, clearing everything out of sight. He'd only just finished when Alysa came in slowly.

She was wearing the towelling robe, and walked hesitantly, as if in a daze. For a moment Drago wondered if she knew who he was.

'Warmer now?' he asked.

She nodded and he moved cautiously forward, brushing her cheeks, which were still wet.

'You haven't dried your face properly,' he said.

But he realised with a shock that she was still weeping—not in gasps and sobs, but quietly, endlessly.

He didn't waste time asking what the matter was. He guessed that this was rooted in the grim, emotionless front she'd presented when she'd learned about Carlotta's pregnancy, and in the explosion that had made her destroy Carlotta's things. He didn't understand anything, and he knew that only patience would help him now.

'Go to bed,' he said. 'And keep warm. No—' He stopped her as she turned to the bed. 'Not in that robe. It's damp.'

'I haven't got anything else.'

'Then I'll get you something.'

He returned after a moment with one of his own shirts.

'It's thick, for winter,' he said. 'I'll be back in a minute.'

She stared at the shirt while tears streamed, unheeded, down her cheeks. Her brain was moving slowly, realising at last that she was meant to take off the robe and put on the shirt. She did so, but then remembered that there was something else to be done. Yes: get into bed. She managed that, and was lying staring at the ceiling when he returned with a glass of brandy.

'Drink this,' he commanded, raising her with one arm and holding the glass to her lips with the other hand.

She obeyed without protest, which worried him more than anything. When he laid her back down, her tears were still flowing.

'Tell me about it,' he said. 'I want to know everything. It's not just the baby, is it? There's something more.'

'Baby,' she whispered. 'Baby…baby…'

'Yes, neither of us thought of her being pregnant by him,' he said gently.

'Baby—my baby,' she gasped. *My baby!*

At first he thought he hadn't heard properly. Then he saw her hands outside the blanket, placed flat across her stomach as though trying to protect something there—or something that was no longer there.

'Baby—baby!' she screamed. *No, no, no!*

'Alysa, did you have James's baby?'

'I was going to tell him just before Christmas,' she whispered, looking far beyond Drago. 'I was so happy to be carrying his child. I waited for him but he phoned to say he wasn't coming. I thought, just be patient, tell him next time. But when we met he told me about Carlotta, and I couldn't say anything then, could I?'

'You might have reminded him that he had responsibilities.'

'I didn't want his pity,' she said fiercely. 'I didn't want his duty, or to be a responsibility. If he didn't love me any more, there was nothing else.'

'You're right, I'm sorry,' Drago agreed quietly. He brushed her hair back. 'So the bastard made you both pregnant at the same time. He's lucky to be dead. If he was here now I think I'd kill him. What happened to your baby?'

'I lost it. It was just after they died, when I'd found out her full name and was looking her up on the internet. I couldn't stop—night after night—and then one night the pain started, and that was that.'

'Oh, dear lord!' He bowed his head. 'And then

I made you find out about this. Perhaps someone should shoot me. I deserve it.'

'No—you didn't know. But I was all right before today. I didn't really mind very much—it was for the best.'

'You don't mean that.'

'Don't I?' she asked with a small hiccup. 'I'm not sure what I mean any more, but it was what I believed then. I thought I'd cry for ages, but then I found I couldn't cry at all. So I put it behind me.'

But she hadn't, he thought, discovering that he could see into her with shocking clarity. She'd coped by turning herself into a pillar of ice, freezing all emotion because that was the only way she'd been able to bear it. And all the time this had been lying in wait for her.

'Didn't your friends or family help you?' he asked.

'I never told anyone I was pregnant.'

'But wasn't there anybody at home to look after you? Hospitals usually ask about that before they'll discharge you.'

'I didn't go to hospital. It happened at home, on a Friday night. I stayed in bed for the weekend, and on Monday I went back to work.'

'Are you saying that you never told *anyone*?'

'You're the first,' she said simply.

He thought of her in that appalling isolation, and inwardly he shivered. His own loneliness seemed nothing in comparison. At least he'd never awoken to find himself alone in the house. In his bleakest moments he'd been able to go along the corridor, quietly open the door of Tina's room and stand listening to her breathing before retreating, at peace, even if only for a while.

But even that short-lived peace was denied Alysa. She had no child to provide a reason for living. Until this moment he hadn't known he was blessed.

Alysa had turned away from him to bury her face in the pillow, overwhelmed by choking sobs.

'Forgive me,' he said desperately. 'I should never have brought you here. I had no idea—I thought only of myself.'

He reached out to touch her trembling shoulders.

'Alysa, please, talk to me.'

'Go away,' she choked. 'I can't talk—I can't. *Please go away.*'

He could do nothing but leave, although it was the last thing he wanted. If he'd dared he would have put his arms around her and offered her all the comfort in his power, although he knew how inadequate it must be. But all she wanted from him was his absence, so he slipped away.

As he reached his own room his mobile phone was ringing. It was Tina.

'Poppa, I've been ringing and ringing.'

'I'm sorry, little one. It's snowing up here and I got lost in the woods.' It was a feeble excuse, and Tina thought so too because she cackled hilariously.

'*Poppa!* You never get lost.'

'I used to think so too,' he said wryly. 'But I was wrong. I've taken a lot of wrong turnings up here.'

Tina spoke with childish sternness. 'You're talking itty-bitty.'

It meant 'nonsense', and was their private joke.

'Don't be angry with me, *cara*. Are you enjoying yourself at Aunt Maria's?'

'Oh yes, we played hide and seek all over the house, and Nonna was cross, but Aunt Maria said…'

She babbled on innocently for a few minutes, and he sensed with relief that she would be happy for a few days.

'Are you snowed in, Poppa?'

'I'm afraid so. It may be a few days before I can get down.'

'Have you got enough to eat?' she asked like a little housewife.

'Plenty, thank you. The cupboard is full.'

'And you will be careful?'

'Stop nagging me,' he protested, grinning. 'It's time you were in bed.'

'That's what Nonna said, but Aunt Maria says I can stay up, and my uncle wants me to teach him how to play dice better, because I keep beating him, and…'

Her chatter was like balm. He bid her a cheerful goodnight, and hung up.

But his cheerfulness faded as he remembered Alysa and the state he'd reduced her to. After a moment he did as he'd often done with Tina— went to stand at her door, listening. From within came the sounds of violent distress, unabated. He leaned back against the wall, wondering if he dared go inside. She'd banished him, yet she needed him. Torn in two, he couldn't move.

Then the sobbing ceased suddenly, to be replaced by a violent coughing. That did it. He gave up struggling with himself and hurried inside.

The light was off but the curtains were drawn back, and in the moonlight he could see her outline heaving.

'Alysa, sit up,' he said, sitting on the bed and taking hold of her. 'It'll be much easier that way.'

She sat up, holding him for support, then leaned forward, seeming to be torn apart by the coughs that wracked her.

'You stupid woman!' he groaned. 'Going out in that snow. You've caught your death of cold now.'

She couldn't answer, too caught up in her distress to have any breath left.

'I've got to keep you warm,' he muttered. 'Wait here. Don't go away.'

The idiocy of the words struck him before he was out of the door, but he was moving fast, dashing to his bedroom to seize up his own thick dressing-gown, then back to her, ordering, 'Put this on. I'll be right back.'

He returned to find her wearing the dressing gown, but not exactly as he wanted.

'Pull it right across the front to protect your chest,' he commanded, demonstrating. 'Now get back into bed, and drink this.'

He produced another glass of brandy which he

almost poured down her throat. She choked but finished it.

'That's better. Now lie down so that I can pull the bedclothes over you. What's that?'

She was struggling to speak, but another bout of coughing tore her. When she'd calmed down she gasped, 'Made—a mess—of everything.'

'I couldn't have made a bigger mess if I'd tried,' he said with feeling.

'Not you—me. Going out like that.'

'Shut up. The blame is mine and we both know it. What was I thinking of? I should have read those letters first instead of just dumping them on you.'

'Makes no difference,' she said in a hoarse whisper. 'You couldn't have known about my baby. Not your fault.'

'Don't be generous,' he begged. 'It makes me feel worse. I'd rather you yelled at me.'

'Can't—no breath.'

He managed a brief laugh. 'Then chuck something at my head. Shall I find you a heavy object?'

'No energy—consider it chucked.' The words ended in another coughing fit. 'Oh dear,' she said.

'I agree. Wait a minute, I've just thought of something.'

He left and returned after a few minutes with a bottle and spoon.

'We always kept medicine up here, just in case. I wasn't sure there was any left after all this time. This is good cough-mixture. Open your mouth.'

She let him coax her until she'd swallowed some, and felt it soothing her as it went down.

'Now lie down and try to get to sleep,' he said as he'd said so often to his child. Right this minute, that was how he felt about Alysa—she was his to protect.

Alysa lay back, exhausted from coughing and weeping. She no longer had the energy to do anything except sink into the warmth and let the world fade away. She was safe, as she hadn't been for a long time, and it was blissful to let go.

'I'm OK now,' she murmured. 'You don't have to mother-hen me.'

'Just go to sleep.'

She closed her eyes at once.

Hours later she awoke in the same position, feeling rested after a dreamless sleep. She stretched, and discovered that she was not alone on the bed. Drago lay just behind her, fully dressed and outside the bedclothes, evidently taking his nursing duties seriously.

'Mother hen,' she said tenderly.

Moving carefully, not wanting to disturb him, she eased herself out of the bed and made her way to the bathroom. When she returned Drago was lying in the same position, except that his arm was stretched out over the space she had occupied, as though he'd been searching for her. She contrived to slide in underneath his arm without disturbing him, and held quite still in case he should awake. He seemed dead to the world, but after a moment his arm tightened around her. She slept.

CHAPTER SEVEN

WHEN Alysa next awoke she was alone, and the sound of frying was coming from the kitchen. She made haste to get up, although she felt feverish, and another coughing fit attacked her. She took some more of the medicine, noting with dismay that the bottle was now empty.

'You sound bad,' Drago said as soon as she appeared in the kitchen.

'I'm all right, really. That medicine is good but I seem to have finished it.'

'Don't worry, there's another bottle. I'll make you some coffee. Sit down.'

He served her eggs, bacon and delicious coffee, smiling briefly when he looked at her, which wasn't often. She had the sense that he was uncomfortable in her company, and wondered if he was simply embarrassed at the position in which he found himself. He hadn't brought her here to nurse her through a childish ailment.

'I'm sorry,' she said after only a few mouthfuls. 'I can't eat very much.'

'I think you should go back to bed.' He touched her forehead with the back of his hand. 'You're feverish. Go on.'

He was right, and she was glad to lie down again. But it was strange that he sounded almost curt, as though he couldn't get rid of her fast enough.

When she awoke the light had changed, becoming duller. She sat up, listening to the silence of the house, and feeling suddenly fearful.

Not to worry, she thought, getting out of bed. She would find Drago and all would be well. But as she moved through room after room a nameless dread began to take hold of her. He was nowhere to be found.

Keep calm, she told herself. He must be somewhere.

But every door she opened only revealed more emptiness, and the dread began to envelop her. Looking out of the window, she saw the mountains rearing up, covered in snow, a white hell into which he had disappeared.

The car; he might have taken it.

But when she descended to the garage the car was still there. Drago hadn't merely gone away. He'd vanished into thin air.

She stood, nonplussed, wondering what was going to happen now. She was alone, abandoned in a strange country, trapped by the snow, and she didn't feel up to doing anything except going back to bed. She ought to be strong-minded, but how would that help?

'Are you out of your mind?'

Drago's shout, coming out of nowhere, made her jump and turn to see him coming in through the garage door, enveloping her in an icy blast.

'What the devil are you doing out here, dressed like that?' he yelled. 'Get back inside.'

'I just—'

'Go in before you catch pneumonia.'

He took hold of her arm, hustling her inside and up the stairs, muttering furiously.

'Why do I bother looking after you if you have no common sense?'

'You vanished. It worried me.'

'I went to get you some more cough mixture. I thought we had another bottle, but I was wrong, so

I went down to the village. I had to walk because the car wouldn't be safe in these conditions.'

'You walked all the way down there and back in the snow?'

'Yes, and for what? For a dimwit who hasn't the sense to keep warm when she's sick. If you die of pneumonia, I'll really lose patience with you.'

She gave a husky laugh, which brought on another fit of coughing.

'I've got you some pills as well. Have a couple now, and some cough mixture, then go back to bed while I get the place warmer and fix you something to eat. And stand away from me. I don't want your germs.'

She eyed him satirically. 'And they say chivalry is dead.'

'This isn't chivalry, it's self-protection. Just do as I say.'

She took the medicine and went thankfully back to her room. But before getting into bed she looked out of the window at the mountains, which were already becoming shadowy as the early-winter dusk began to fall. Down below she saw a door open, and Drago appear, heading for the woodshed. He emerged with his arms full of logs, which he carried into the house. A few moments later he made another journey to fetch charcoal.

Then sounds came from along the corridor, telling her that he was refilling the range, causing the house to grow warmer at once, or so it seemed to her.

But the consoling warmth had little to do with the heating. Drago had returned, and the demons that had haunted her for the last year were in retreat. Comforted, she climbed into bed and snuggled beneath the covers.

He brought her some soup, and a cup of coffee, both of which he set down at a careful distance.

'Eat that even if you aren't hungry,' he said brusquely. 'I don't want you starving to death either. You'd do it just to be awkward.'

'Then why don't you just throw me out of the window and get it over with?' she demanded huskily. 'Think of the trouble you'd save.'

He appeared to consider this before saying, 'Too difficult to explain away the body. It suits me better if you stay alive.'

'Gosh, thanks!'

He gave her a ribald grin before vanishing.

The grin faded as soon as he was out of her

sight. He'd been on edge since he'd awoken that morning, to find himself lying with his arm over her. It wasn't what he'd meant to happen. He'd stayed with her the night before out of concern and a desire to be on hand if she needed him. When sleep had overcome him he'd lain down beside her, careful to stay outside the bedclothes, not touching her.

He wasn't sure exactly when he'd put his arm over her, but he must have done so, because he'd been holding her when he awoke. At all costs she mustn't find out. In their special circumstances it was a betrayal of trust. He could only be thankful that he'd awoken first, and had escaped without discovery.

Even so, he'd been on edge when she'd got up, waiting to detect any hint of suspicion in her manner, but there'd been nothing. She'd merely looked bedraggled and vulnerable, a different woman from the austere female he'd met only three days ago. But that had only increased his feeling of guilt, and he'd taken refuge in a surly manner.

It was almost a relief to discover that the medicine had run out, so that he'd had to take a long walk down to the village through the snow. He'd looked in to tell her he was going but, finding her asleep, had slipped quietly away.

He'd hoped the walk would clear his head, but his confusions merely settled into a different pattern. The discovery that his wife had been pregnant by her lover had shattered him, but he'd been prepared for new pain. What he hadn't anticipated was Alysa's agony.

If asked to describe himself he would have refused, then done it unwillingly: a straightforward man who loved his family, but without frills or fine words. That was him. Empathy was something for others, those with time to waste.

But Alysa's suffering had torn through him, so that he felt it with her. It was a new sensation, and if he was honest he didn't like it. From now on he would simply help her recover, pray for the snow to melt, and bid her goodbye with relief. Above all he'd decided he would behave with circumspection, and speak to her with the greatest care.

But that was before he'd arrived home to find her in the freezing garage, and his explosion of temper had banished good resolutions to the far ends of the earth. Having seen her safely in bed, he stormed into the kitchen and got to work in a fury. As he prepared the meal they would eat that evening, he lashed his anger to keep it alive, because that way he might avoid the thoughts and feelings lying in wait for him.

He scowled when she finally emerged into the kitchen, still in his robe.

'Are you sure you're ready to get up?' he growled.

'Yes, I feel better now. Those pills you got me are good.'

'Go and sit by the fire while I finish making supper.'

'Can't I—?'

'Do as you're told.'

'Yes, *sir*!'

Her office colleagues would laugh if they could see her now, she thought, curling up on the rug by the fire and tossing on some more wood. She was famed for her cool head and ability to organise. But right now it was nice to be waited on.

Supper was steak and red wine, which he brought to her by the fire, and they picnicked like children. It was the best steak she'd ever tasted.

'I feel guilty that you had to go out for me,' she said.

'I'm the one who feels guilty, trapping you up here without even a change of clothes.'

'Look,' she said awkwardly. 'About what I did to Carlotta's things…'

'Did you really do all that?' he asked, fascinated.

'Every last slash.'

'Did it make you feel any better?'

'Much,' she said, with such feeling that he grinned. 'I'm sorry, Drago, I know you must have treasured them.'

'If I did I was a sentimental fool. I should have done what you did long ago. Have you kept any souvenirs of James?'

'I may have something lying around. It's a while since I looked.' She saw his wry look and said, 'All right, I still have one of his shirts. He was wearing it the day he said he loved me— at least, he didn't actually say that. Now I think of it, he phrased it very carefully, but at the time…' She sighed. 'I guess I heard what I wanted to hear.'

'Yes, we do that when we're very much in love.'

'And you were, weren't you? Very much.'

'I didn't think it was possible to love a woman as much as I loved her,' he said slowly. 'We met on every level—mentally, physically, everything. No matter how often I made love to her it wasn't enough. In bed she was never the same woman twice, and I always wanted more of her.'

'How long were you married?'

'Ten years.'

'And all that love you spoke of—it was still there, wasn't it?'

'As much as on the first day,' he said slowly. 'And she loved me the same way. I would have sworn it. Until she met him, and he changed her.'

'So you blame James?'

'I hate him,' Drago said simply. 'I don't hate him any less because he's dead. I'm glad he's dead. I hope he suffered agonies. I hate him as much as you must hate Carlotta, or you couldn't have carved up her clothes. If she'd been there herself, I dread to think what you'd have done to her.'

'Maybe. I blamed her for taking him from me, but I wonder if she could have done that if he hadn't been willing.'

He didn't answer, and she looked up to find him staring into the fire.

'It works both ways,' he said at last. 'You're saying that she must have been willing too, but I don't believe that.'

'Perhaps she was a little restless. Maybe she just meant to have a minor flirtation and it got out of hand.'

'*No*. She didn't flirt. At parties I used to watch her. She'd laugh and tease the men, but there was a line she never crossed. And nor did I. We had a wonderful marriage until she met him.'

'But did you know what she was thinking? Do we ever know, no matter how close we think we are?'

He grimaced. 'You mean I was fooling myself then, and I'm still doing it now? Maybe you're right and I just don't have your courage. I want to keep my memories. Nothing so beautiful will ever happen to me again, and I can't let it go.'

'You still love her.'

'No,' he said quickly. 'The love is dead, but it was glorious while it lasted, and I can't just consign it to the rubbish heap. If I have to live with dreams for the rest of my life, I'll do it rather than live without them.'

She regarded him in wonder. On the surface this big, powerful man was armoured against anything the world could do to him. The truth was hidden away inside his heart, in a place so secret that even he feared to visit it often.

He understood her look, and said, 'I've never told that to anyone but you.'

'And I'll never repeat it,' she promised.

'Thank you. I know I can trust you.'

As he said it he looked away from her. But then he looked back, and the trust he spoke of was there in his eyes, communicating directly without words.

He must have looked at Carlotta like that—with total, defenceless confidence. Only two people in the world had seen it. Carlotta was one, and she was the other. It felt strange to have something in common with that woman.

'I think you're right to keep your dreams of her,' she said. 'If only for Tina's sake.'

'What about you?' he asked. 'Is there anyone for whose sake you have to keep quiet?'

'Nobody.'

The word fell on him like stone, and he recalled what she'd told him of the bleakness of her life. Not that she would call it bleak. She would simply say she was organised.

He moved beside her and put his arms about her, holding her tight.

'You'll get my germs,' she protested.

'To hell with them.'

After a while she asked sleepily, 'Are there many more letters to read?'

He pulled over the bag so that several envelopes fell onto the floor. They each took some and began riffling through them. Alysa opened one in James's handwriting and read:

I never believed in the kind of love you hear about in songs, until I met you, and you showed me it could happen. Before that, I always settled for the easy version of love that I could take or leave. I never risked the kind that tears out a man's heart and tells him he'd be better dead than losing his woman. But then I met you and knew that you were that woman. You gave me courage. Bless you for that, my darling.

She stared into the fire until she saw Drago looking at her, and handed the letter to him.

'"Better dead",' Drago read aloud. 'He didn't know what he was saying.'

'He was never like that with me,' she murmured. 'He was always cheerful, funny— even when we— And it was nice sometimes.' She broke off to sneeze.

'Don't force yourself,' Drago said gently.

'I used to think it would be lovely if he was a bit more romantic, but I told myself that he just couldn't find the right words, and he loved me really. But the way he wrote to Carlotta—all passion and intensity—it's like a different man. I guess I never really knew him, because he didn't want me to.'

'I was luckier than you,' Drago admitted. 'Whatever Carlotta did at the end, I know who she was in the years before—the woman who gave me all herself. Nothing can change that.'

'Good,' she said with sudden decisiveness. 'Hold onto that thought. It'll stop you becoming a psycho like me.'

'You're not a psycho.'

'I was headed that way. I can see it now. I

deadened my heart because I thought it would be easier. But it wasn't. Listen to your friend, Drago. Don't become like me.'

He grinned tenderly. 'If my daughter could hear you now. You really took her advice to heart.'

'You mean about looking after you?'

'Yes, you're doing a great job.'

'Then we're even.'

She didn't know how long they sat there on the floor, leaning against each other, but she could happily have stayed for ever. It wasn't thrilling or dramatic, or any of the things she had known with James. But every moment that passed was healing something deep inside her, bringing her back to life.

And him too. That thought made her almost happy. Let him put Carlotta on a pedestal if that was what he needed. She wouldn't spoil it for him.

'Time you were in bed,' he announced suddenly. 'I'll make you a hot chocolate and you can take your pills.'

While he was in the kitchen she took another

letter. It was from Carlotta, and she read it with little more than casual interest. She was beginning to feel that nothing else could happen.

Within a few lines she discovered her mistake. Carlotta had written:

We made a pact to be honest with each other, so I'm going to tell you the complete truth. You asked if you were my first lover since my marriage, and, though I'd love to say yes, the truth is that there have been others.

Alysa's hands tightened on the paper so that it crumpled. When she'd flattened it she read it again, wondering if she'd misunderstood. But there was no mistaking what Carlotta was saying.

I know now that I married before I was quite ready. It was thrilling to defy my mother with an elopement, and Drago was insistent, so I yielded unwisely.

I should have lived a more exciting life before I settled down. I realised soon after the wedding that domesticity bored me, so I compensated with a few little 'adventures'.

'Bitch,' Alysa muttered, barely aware that she was speaking.

Drago never found out. I did my best to be a good wife to him in other ways, and I gave him Tina, whom he adores. So I don't really feel guilty.

My love, never fear. To you I will be faithful. With you I find a completeness and a fulfilment that I never found with Drago.

Here it was, the proof that Drago was fooling himself. Far from being the woman who had given him all of herself, she'd shared herself out pretty freely, it seemed. He'd endured her betrayal and loss, but this would break his heart finally.

A sound from the kitchen made her stuff the letter back into the envelope. It was instinctive. Without thinking about it, she knew she wasn't going to show him this.

'Anything interesting?' he asked, coming in and setting down the hot chocolate.

'No, just more of the same,' she said casually. 'Oh, that looks lovely.'

He gathered up the letters and tossed them back into the bag.

'Enough of them for tonight,' he said.

He pushed the bag onto a low shelf. Alysa watched, blaming herself for not taking the letter while she'd had the chance. Now she could do nothing without arousing his suspicion.

She maintained a calm façade as she bid him goodnight and retired to bed. She even managed to sleep for a while. But then she awoke, every nerve on edge, knowing that she must secure that letter before he saw it.

She might argue with herself that it was illogical for her to protect him, but this wasn't logic. This was emotion, a luxury she hadn't allowed herself for too long. Drago had said he trusted her, and what happened to him now was in her hands.

Moving silently, she got out of bed and looked out into the corridor. The house was silent, and no light could be seen beneath Drago's door. This was her one chance. It took a few seconds to creep into the main room where there was still a faint glow from the dying fire, locate the bag on the shelf and speed back to her room.

A quick search revealed the cruel letter. She read it briefly to make sure it was the right one, then slipped it into the drawer of her bedside locker. Feverishly she began searching through the remaining letters, just in case there was another mention of Carlotta's infidelity. She found it in James's reply, and took that too. When she was sure she'd removed everything dangerous, she slipped back into the corridor and stood in the darkness, listening fearfully. But there was no sound.

Then a quick dash to replace the bag where Drago had left it. It was done. Now all she had to do was get back to her room. She was almost there when she heard his door opening, and turned, standing petrified in the light of the window.

Then she saw something that shocked her. A smile illuminated Drago's face, so that for a moment it was brilliant with joy. His hand moved as if to reach out to her, but then it fell back to his side and the smile died.

'Are you all right?' he asked politely.

'Yes—yes. I just had to—get up for a minute. Goodnight.'

She fled to her room and stood leaning against the door, trying not to believe what had happened: for a split second in the darkness Drago had thought she was Carlotta. He'd smiled, almost reaching out to her. But then the smile had died as the sad truth had overcome him again.

Now Alysa was passionately glad at what she had done. It was wrong, disgraceful. She was a thief. But she had protected him from further grief, and she wasn't sorry.

She could hear him moving about in his bedroom next door to hers, and the mysterious communication that seemed to unite them showed her his movements—from the door to the window and back again, from the door to the wall, to the window.

A pause, then the sound of the window being opened. In her mind she could see him standing there, looking out at the dark mountains with the moon rising behind them, trying to cool himself in the chill air. Vainly seeking an elusive peace.

She knew the moment when he closed the

window and began to pace the room again, until he ended up by the wall that separated him from her. She held her breath, hoping he'd gone to bed.

But then came the sound of a long groan, like an animal caught in a trap. It shivered away into nothing, and after that there was silence.

CHAPTER EIGHT

FOR the next couple of days they continued going through the letters, but there were no more revelations, and at last they could relax. The pills worked well and her cold improved fast, until they were able to go out for a breath of fresh air. Drago acted like a nanny, making her wear his own coat, and buttoning it up to the throat, while she laughed with pleasure. It was bliss to be fussed over.

'You're twice my size,' she said, regarding herself in the mirror, almost vanishing into the huge coat, and flapping the sleeves which hung comically off the ends of her arms. 'Whatever do I look like?'

'You look like someone who needs a scarf,' he said, wrapping one around her neck several times. 'Has nobody ever taken any care of you?'

'My mother did, until she died. But after that I've been pretty independent.'

For 'independent' read 'alone', he thought.

'What about James?' he wanted to know.

She made a face. James hadn't been the protective kind, and until this moment it hadn't bothered her.

The beauty of the mountain was overwhelming as they went carefully up the slope, Alysa clinging to his arm at his insistence to avoid slipping. Overhead the trees hung heavy with snow, while in front of them the white path led up out of sight.

'I've never seen anything so lovely,' she sighed.

'Don't you have snow in England?'

'It turns to sludge very quickly. But this…'

She let go of his arm and turned round and round, looking up so that the bright morning sun fell on her face. Drago watched her, smiling at her ecstasy.

'You look like a scarecrow,' he said.

'Thank you, kind sir. Yes, I do, don't I?' She began to spin faster. *'Wheee!'*

'You're scaring the birds,' he protested as a

startled flock rose from the branches above, fleeing these wild noises.

The next moment they were engulfed in snow that had been disturbed by the scattering birds. Alysa collapsed with laughter, leaning back against a tree and sliding down.

'Don't sit on the ground, you crazy woman,' Drago said, brushing snow out of his hair and taking hold of her.

He yanked her unceremoniously to her feet, so that she staggered and he had to steady her against him.

'Behave,' he told her firmly. 'Are you totally intent on getting pneumonia?'

'That would be very awkward for you,' she laughed. 'Especially if I died. You get me up here, and I vanish for ever. You could be in big trouble.'

'Nonsense, they'd give me a medal. Now, come on, I want to get you safely into the warm.'

'Suppose I want to stay?'

His answer was to pick her up and march firmly back to the villa.

'Why do some women argue about everything?' he growled.

'Some men are made to be argued with,' she

said, steadying herself with both arms around his neck. 'The temptation is irresistible.'

He gave a bark of laughter, turning his head to glance at her, and immediately wished he hadn't. Her mouth was so close to his that their lips almost touched. He looked ahead quickly, shaken by the vibration that went through him, almost causing him to stumble, and feeling her arms tighten about his neck.

'Steady,' she said in a trembling voice. 'I don't want to be dumped on the ground again.'

'I'm sorry,' he said huskily.

She struggled to control her breathing, which was coming in awkward jerks, thankful that he couldn't sense the beating of her heart. Or could he? She could sense his. Unless it was merely the echo of her own.

Don't overreact. It was over a year since a man's lips had touched her own, and she'd been taken by surprise.

As he strode on she watched the side of his face. It was dark with something that she might have mistaken for fury if she hadn't known better. She had neither fear nor hope that he would follow through; not now, while she was dependent on him. It would be a betrayal of trust, and he was a man of honour. There was no justice in the world, she thought sadly.

As soon as they reached home they got to work, stoking up the fire, working in the kitchen, managing to avoid each other's eyes even when they said goodnight and retired to their rooms.

That night it rained, and by morning the worst of the snow had gone. Drago said he would arrange for her bags to be delivered. To her relief his manner was normal again, and she was able to respond in the same tone.

'I've managed well enough so far,' she said with a gleam of humour. 'Although I suppose I should stop pinching your shirts.'

'That's the third one you're wearing. I'll be glad for you to recover your own clothes before I run out.'

Then his smile died. 'But it's not that. The truth is that these last few days have been— Didn't you feel it?'

'Oh yes,' she said in a tone of wonder. 'We laughed. Can you believe that? I don't think I've laughed in months.'

'Me neither. It was the last thing I was expecting when we came here. It's you—I've never known anyone like you. I don't want this time to end.'

'Neither do I,' she admitted.

'Just a couple more days?'

'All right.'

'I'll call home and get them to send the bags right away.'

But before he could take out his mobile phone, Alysa's own telephone shrilled, startling her. The sound seemed to come from another world, one she had left behind without regret. The caller was her boss.

'Alysa? Are you all right? I got worried when we didn't hear from you.'

'I'm fine, Brian,' she said, trying to sound bright. 'I took a little trip into the mountains and got snowed in.'

'Damn. There are big things happening here, and it would really help if you came back.'

'But I left everything in good order. I even cleared up all the problems with the Riley account.'

'I know, and he's very impressed,' Brian admitted. 'So impressed that he's introduced a new client and told him to ask for you and nobody else. But he wants an early appointment. You should be very proud.'

'Yes,' she said slowly. 'I suppose I should.'

His voice changed, became persuasive.

'Mind you, if it's really difficult, I suppose I could assign him to someone else. Frank's proving very good.'

She knew Frank, a newcomer who was straining every nerve to impress the boss, and would obliterate her if he could. Brian had known just what to say.

'How's the snow?' he asked.

'Clearing,' she admitted reluctantly. 'All right, I'll be back tomorrow.'

Drago was watching her as she hung up.

'Duty calls?' he asked wryly.

'I guess it does. Oh, if only—'

'Hey, that's enough. If there's one thing you and I have learned not to say, it's "if only".'

'I can't help it. If only—if only—'

She wondered what was happening to her. It had been on the tip of her tongue to tell Brian that she was still trapped and needed more time. But the habit of putting work first was too strong, and the words had come out of their own accord.

'There's a flight at six o'clock this evening,' Drago said. 'I'll book it for you.'

Her heart sank. She wanted to say that tomorrow would have done, and they could have spent one last comfortable evening together. Now it was too late. Unless, perhaps, there were no seats. But even that hope died.

'All fixed,' Drago said, hanging up.

'I should have put Brian off,' she said unhappily. 'I wanted those extra days.'

'So did I, but it wasn't to be, and maybe it's best. We've had something we both needed, and we're stronger for it. I shall be glad for the rest of my life that I met you, and you helped me survive.'

He reached out, enveloping her in a bear hug against the warmth of his chest. She turned her head so that it rested on his shoulder with her face turned away from him. His words reminded her of the letter she'd taken and which now, more than ever, she was determined that he must never see. She was afraid to meet his eyes lest they should somehow reveal her thoughts.

They had been granted a special time in which to heal each other's wounds. It had brought them suffering, but also a kind of healing. Now it was time to move on to a life that might be bearable again. But still her heart ached.

Drago called his home and arranged for her luggage to be delivered to the airport, while she went to pack up the few things she had with her, putting the dangerous letter firmly away in her bag.

He made her a final meal of spaghetti, and they washed up together.

'We'd better leave now,' he said. 'I'll need to drive slowly.'

They made it to the foot of the mountain without mishap, and then they were on the road to the airport. Once there he bought her a coffee and went to meet the chauffeur, returning a few minutes later with her suitcases.

'We've got a few minutes before you need to check in,' he said, sitting down with her at the table.

'Yes.'

Just a few minutes, and then she might never see him again. The speed of her departure had taken her by surprise. There were so many things she wanted to say to him, but suddenly she couldn't remember any of them, and the time was ticking past.

A waiter asked if Drago wanted anything, and

he asked for coffee without taking his eyes off Alysa. When it came he didn't even notice.

'That's that, then,' he said.

'Yes.'

'It should be a calm flight. The weather's cleared nicely.'

'Yes,' she said again.

She wanted to meet his gaze, yet she feared to meet it. There was something there that she couldn't afford to see now that she was leaving. He was her friend and comfort, both of which she needed too much to risk them with any other kind of relationship. And yet—and yet...

'Call me when you get there,' he said. 'Just to let me know you've landed safely.'

'Yes,' she said for the fourth time. Inwardly she was cursing herself for being tongue-tied.

'Yes,' he echoed heavily.

She gave him a faint smile. 'I reckon we've exhausted the conversation.'

'It's not the words,' he said. 'It's the other things.'

'Yes,' she said before she could stop herself, and they both laughed awkwardly.

'Luckily the other things don't need saying,' he added.

As he spoke he reached out across the table to take her hand in his, rubbing his thumb softly across the backs of her fingers, then raising them so that he could brush them across his cheek. When he released her he put his hand to his eyes for a moment.

'Will you be all right, after everything I've put you through?' he asked.

'Don't worry, I'm tough.'

He met her eyes. His own were gentle.

'No,' he said softly. 'You're not.'

'You're not either.'

He gave the self-mocking smile that touched her heart. 'Don't tell anyone.'

'I promise. It'll be our secret. What about you? Will *you* be all right?'

'I will now, with your help. I'm only sorry it was so hard on you. I got off lightly in comparison.'

She thought of the letter that he must never see, and smiled at him.

'Drago, I'm not sorry we met. I'll never regret that, however hard it was.'

'Nor I.' He looked down and spoke awkwardly. 'In some ways I'm glad I didn't meet you earlier, when I was still married to Carlotta. There would have been…problems.'

'I know,' she whispered.

'We'd better be moving.'

He waited while she checked in, then came to the barrier with her.

'This is as far as I can go,' he said.

But that wasn't what he really meant; she knew. It was as far as they could go together.

'Goodbye, Drago.'

'Goodbye.'

For a moment she thought he would kiss her, but instead he pulled her close for a fierce embrace, which she went into willingly. Holding him, feeling him hold her, she told herself that this was the last time she would seek refuge in him, and feel him seek it in her. And a tide of regret swept over her.

'That's your flight they're calling,' he said with a sudden husky note in his voice. 'You'd better hurry.'

But he didn't release her.

'Yes, I suppose I must.'

'Hey, are you crying?'

'Yes,' she choked.

She tightened her arms again, then released him and moved away quickly. As she went through Passport Control, she wiped her tears and took a last glance back at him, blaming herself for being glad he was still there. Then the check on her hand luggage. Another few moments and he would be out of her life for ever.

One final look. Just one. And there was his hand raised in farewell, and his smile seeming to call her back.

And that was it, she thought. That was the mystery about their brief time together—every moment of it a contradiction of the moment before, each truth denying the others. She'd been drawn to him from the first, even while she'd raged at him. He'd made her stronger. She could only hope that she had done the same for him.

It was evening when the plane touched down, and the cold struck her as soon as she was outside. It was different from the cold of the mountains, which had been fresh and invigorating. This was merely depressing.

The queue for the taxi took ages, and she took the chance to call him.

'Safely down,' she said.

'Good. I'd say go home and have a good rest, but I guess there'll be a pile of messages waiting for you there.'

'I'd rather be back in the mountains.'

'So would I— One moment.'

Alysa could hear Tina calling in the background. So she was home now, and naturally wanted her father's attention after having been away from him.

'I have to go,' she said. 'Goodbye. And thank you for everything.'

'Goodbye, Alysa—and thank you.'

To her relief the taxi came, and she could force her mind back to the present and the future. Gradually the lights of London enfolded her again, and she told herself that it was good to come home. She said that several times.

Her apartment was chilly. As soon as she entered she saw a light winking on her phone, telling her that there was a message. She picked it up and found it was Brian.

'Welcome back. I knew I could rely on you. I've made an appointment with your new client for tomorrow afternoon. That'll give me time to brief you in the morning. Frank's furious that he couldn't steal a march on you. I thought you'd enjoy that. Get a good night's sleep and be ready for action.'

She switched off and looked around the empty apartment, seeing it with new eyes. How bare it was! How long had it been like that? And she hadn't noticed. It spoke of a woman who hardly existed, inside whose heart nothing happened.

She wondered what Drago was doing now.

Next day Frank scowled to see her back, which really was satisfying. She listened to Brian's briefing, taking in every word, and when she met the client that afternoon everything went well. On the surface it was just as before.

But later, when Brian had finished praising her, he added, considering her, 'You've changed. I can't quite work out how, but it's good. I have great hopes of you, Alysa.'

As winter faded into spring, and then into summer, she took on more clients, worked hard and won approving looks from her employers. Unlike Brian, few people were perceptive enough to discern the difference. Her apartment would have given a clue, becoming less stark and functional, but the real change was in her mind and heart, both of which seemed to flower again.

One night she took home a tape-recording of a conference that had been held within the firm eight months previously, wanting to check whether she had really said what the notes stated.

The sound of her own voice made her lean back in her chair, shocked. It might have been a machine talking, so dead and cold did she sound. Now she knew what Drago had heard, and why he had feared for her.

He was with her—unseen, unheard, but a constant pres-ence. She had only to think of him to feel safe again, as though his arms were still holding her. With James there had been a constant yearning for a man who, she now realised, had never really been there. But she did not miss Drago, for how could you miss someone who was always with you?

At last a letter came from him.

I wanted you to know how different things are with me since you were here. Not all the ghosts have been laid to rest, but the worst of them leave me in peace now. I sleep at night, and when I awake I confront the day ahead without despair.

I once thought this could never happen, but now I know that there is one person who knows and understands, and that knowledge is enough to give me strength. Even if we never meet again, you are still here with me in spirit, and you give me the courage I need. I hope with all my heart that it is the same with you.

God bless you.

She wrote back.

You brought me back to life. I had become dead inside, and would have stayed that way always, but for you. It's a strange and con- fusing feeling to reawaken, and I don't yet know who this new person is. But, whoever she is, you made her free to grieve and one day, perhaps soon, she will be well again. For this you will always be dear to me.

He did not write again, nor did she expect him to. They had set each other on a new path, but it led away into the unknown, and they must travel it separately. Sometimes she remembered his words—that he was glad they had not met before because she would have threatened his loyalty to his wife. Who knew where that road might have led? But not yet. Perhaps not ever.

Her sleep, once so blank, had begun to be troubled with dreams. James seemed to haunt her as he'd never done before. She would see his face in that last meeting, but when she approached him he always vanished.

'Where are you?' she cried. 'Where are you?'

But when she awoke to find herself sitting up in bed she knew that she hadn't been calling to James, but to someone else, and that he was already with her. Then she would lie down and sleep again in peace.

She began studying him again on the internet, and soon managed to access Italian newspapers, including one that was local to Florence. It was a ready source of information, as excitement was rising about a mediaeval church that Drago was restoring. Work had slowed the previous year owing to many unexpected problems, but now things were moving again, as Drago seemed infused with new inspiration. It had caused him to insist on changing things that had previously seemed settled, replacing them with better ideas.

There were pictures, showing her the building before Drago had started work—tired-looking and down-at-heel. Now as it neared completion she could see its magnificence restored through his genius, and she felt a sudden happiness, for she thought she knew the source of his new life.

An increase of work left her no time to follow his progress for a while, and it was almost a week before she was able to seek him out on-line. Then she saw something that almost made her heart stop:

Di Luca critical after near-death plunge.

Struggling through the Italian prose, Alysa managed to understand that Drago had climbed high on some scaffolding, intent on examining a carved stone to make sure that it was perfect, had missed his footing and had plunged down to the ground.

It was dated five days ago. He could be dead by now.

Frantically she searched through the following

days, terrified lest she find the fatal announce-
ment. There was nothing, but she searched again,
and this time she spotted a small item saying
that he'd regained consciousness and seemed
better. She read it over and over, terrified that
she'd misread it.

To her relief there had been no mistake, but she
couldn't rest until she knew more. After a few
minutes, summoning up her courage, she lifted
the phone and dialled his home.

Who would answer? she wondered. The
housekeeper? Or perhaps Elena was there again?
She was still running through the possibilities
when Drago's voice said, *'Pronto.'*

At first she was too startled to speak and he had
to say it again before she answered.

'It's me.'

She wondered if she should identify herself
properly, but he recognised 'me' at once.

'Ciao, Alysa. How nice to hear from you.'

Trying to pull herself together, she blurted out,
'What are you doing there? You're supposed to
be at death's door.'

'Is that disappointment I hear in your voice?'
He sounded amused.

'Of course not. They said you'd had a terrible fall and took days to regain consciousness.'

'As usual, the press exaggerates. My fall was broken by a ledge. I had a slight concussion and a couple of cracked ribs, but that's all. I left hospital yesterday. Tomorrow I'll go back to work.'

'With cracked ribs?' she echoed, aghast.

'Why not? They're painful, but I can still bark orders and be generally overbearing.'

'And climb scaffolding?'

'No, not that. I'll be careful, but I have to be there to make sure that everything is done the way I want.'

'That sounds like you,' she said, feeling her heart slow to a more normal rhythm.

'Slave-driver?'

'Perfectionist. Everyone says you're doing a wonderful job on that church.'

'I hope so. It must be finished soon. I've made so many changes recently that it held things up, but we're nearly there. Tell me, how did you know what had happened?'

'The internet. I can access the local Florence paper, and it was all there.'

She paused, embarrassed by what she had just revealed.

For a few moments there was silence from the other end. Then he said, 'You're not so easy to trace. There's your firm's website, which has just a little about you. And a picture of you at some official dinner last week. That's all.'

So he'd been watching her from a distance too. She smiled.

'What kind of a function was it?' he asked casually.

'Like you said, official. Accountants, lawyers, businessmen, a few politicians, lots of boring speeches.'

'You didn't seem bored by the man sitting next to you. You were sharing a laugh.'

'That's my boss, Brian. He thinks he's a wit, so I guess I play up.'

'Ah, the one who can make you a partner?'

'That's right.'

'Then you were right to laugh. Was the joke any good?'

'I can't remember.'

'That's handy. You'll be able to laugh again next time he tells it.'

His voice was warm, turning the remark into a friendly joke, so that she could say, 'I might just do that.'

'You've grown your hair. It's nicer this way.'

'I wonder why I did,' she said lightly. 'Someone may have suggested it, but I can't remember who.'

He laughed but stopped at once.

'Don't make me laugh. It hurts.'

'Please, Drago, I wish you wouldn't go back to work yet. Give yourself a few more days.'

'All right. Just a couple more days. Because you say so.'

'Thank you.'

Then his voice changed, becoming gentler. 'Alysa—how are things with you?'

'I'm managing better now.'

'So am I. Thank you.'

Silence. She felt awkward, and she could sense that he did too.

'Am I forgiven?' he asked at last.

'There's nothing to forgive. You know that.'

'I didn't. But I hoped.'

'Goodbye, Drago.'

'Goodbye.'

The line went dead. Alysa hung up and sat looking at the phone, wondering at the strange feeling that had overtaken her. It was disturbingly like happiness.

So he'd seen her with Brian, and had wondered. But there was nothing romantic in their association, even though he was an outrageously handsome man. A well-preserved fifty-three, he'd been married three times and now determinedly 'avoided shackles'.

He both worked and played hard, but the pleasure was strictly out of office hours. None of his female employees had anything to fear from him, which had caused one of them to mutter that this was because 'the old goat' preferred women who were too stupid to spell, never mind add.

He'd invited Alysa to the dinner as a professional courtesy, introducing her to a lot of influential people, congratulating her on her networking skills, showing the road that led to a partnership. Afterwards he'd taken her home, kissed her on the cheek, and had gone to spend the rest of the night with a lady whose talents were as legendary as her prices.

She wondered if Drago would call her back, or

write, but a month passed with no word from him. Then a large gold envelope came through her door. Opening it, she found an invitation to the ceremonies that would accompany the re-opening of the church he'd been restoring.

The card was practically a work of art in itself, elaborately embossed, the wording formal with nothing personal about it. He'd included a brief note, saying he would book a hotel for her, and inviting her to join him and his other guests at his home the night before the dedication, and again the following evening. It could have been written to almost any guest, but she knew better than to attach importance to its formality.

The true message was that, like her, he longed for another meeting but, also like her, he was cautious. Across the miles his heart and mind reached out to her, as perfectly in harmony as before.

CHAPTER NINE

SHE went to see Brian to ask for a week off.

'I know I've already had a week this year—' she began.

'Hey, don't make me sound like a slave-driver. A week is nothing, and you're due for some time off. Planning anything special?' He looked suddenly alarmed. 'I need you in the firm. You haven't got a lover trying to take you away from us, have you?'

'No, I leave that kind of thing to you,' she teased. 'I'm pursuing business. I met a well-known architect in Italy, and he's invited me to the opening of a church he's just finished restoring.'

'Drago di Luca,' Brian mused, looking at the card. 'I've heard of him. Even in this country he's beginning to be talked about. Well done. If he accepts commissions over here, his business could be valuable.'

She murmured a reply and escaped. He could think she was making a cool move, but the truth was she felt anything but cool.

Drago's chauffeur was waiting to help her at the airport, smiling as he recognised her and took her bags, and handing her an envelope as she got into the car. As he drove her to the same hotel where she'd stayed last time, she opened it and read:

I would have liked to meet you myself but I'm drowning in formalities. You will wish some time alone this afternoon to rest, and a car will collect you at six o'clock and bring you to my home for dinner. Tina is very much looking forward to seeing you again. And so am I.

Once at the hotel, a shower refreshed her so that she had no need of rest. She wanted to go out and see Florence in the sunshine. It was high summer and everything was different, bathed in sunlight. It was hard to believe that this was the same place she'd seen in February, when the cold and damp had seemed to seep into her bones, and become one with her sadness.

Walking down by the river, she watched the light glinting on the water, and was suddenly assailed by a feeling of irrational joy. She tried to be rational. After all, it was only sun. But she didn't want to be rational. She wanted to rejoice in the light and let her steps take her where they would.

At first she thought she was wandering aimlessly, but then she admitted the truth—that she was heading for the apartment where James and Carlotta had briefly lived. She found it easily, and it was looking more cheerful now than it had done in winter. From inside came the sound of laughter, a man's voice, then a woman's, sounding young and happy.

The man might have been James if fate had been kinder to him. But it had not been kind, she thought, from the depths of her new-found peace.

Turning away, she walked on along the river until she came to the Ponte Vecchio, and went to stand before the statue of Cellini, where James and Carlotta had pledged their love with padlocks along with many others. But there were no padlocks there today. The railings that had once been covered with love tokens were stark and bare.

She heard a sigh and turned to see the proprietor of the shop who'd told her the significance of the padlocks, way back in February—a lifetime ago.

'What's happened to them all?' she asked him. 'Don't lovers come here any more?'

'They do when they dare,' he said. 'But the council has ruled against them. If you get caught hanging a padlock there's a fine, and every now and then they clear them all away.'

'That's terrible!'

'Yes, isn't it? Ah well, it all brings me new business.'

'But do people still buy padlocks if they can't hang them?'

'Who says they can't? You don't think lovers let a few fines put them off, do you? Every single one of them who hung a token there before will be back to hang another one. Good day.'

When he'd bustled away, Alysa stood looking at the bare railings.

'Not every single one,' she whispered. 'I lost a

great deal, but I didn't lose everything. *You* lost everything, and I didn't see it until now.'

Again she felt the stirring of pity, and suddenly she knew that there was another place she must see.

A few minutes in a taxi brought her to the Church of All Angels. Like everywhere else it was transformed by the sun, making even the graves look somehow cheerful, especially the monument to Carlotta di Luca, which glowed with a fresh delivery of flowers.

Red roses, Alysa noted: a silent message from Drago that she was still in his heart. She had often wondered if she'd done the right thing in taking the letter, sparing him that pain. Now she thought she had her answer.

At last she wandered over to the far corner where the unimportant graves lay, and there the illusion of cheer was dispelled.

The little slabs had received minimum care. Someone had cut the grass, but casually, so that a fringe of long grass surrounded every slab. Here there were no flowers or tributes. Only the bleakness of indifference. Suddenly James's lonely end seemed intolerable.

It was very quiet in this corner. She stood

looking up at the beauty of the sky, feeling the sun bless her as she had never thought to be blessed again. Overhead a bird began to sing.

'I don't hate you,' she told him sadly. 'How can I, when it all ended so sadly for you? I wish there was something I could— But perhaps there is. If only I knew how to go about it.'

Then a memory returned to her from the day she'd first come here in February—the young journalist talking about Drago, saying, 'They say he has the ear of every important person in town, and he pulls strings whenever it suits him.'

Drago, the dear friend whose support had saved her: she could turn to him again. Suddenly decisive, she left the cemetery and hailed a taxi.

For a party in the elegant surroundings of the villa, she guessed that only grandeur would do, and accordingly chose a long dress of dark-blue satin. The neckline was modest for an evening gown, but the narrow waist hugged her figure, and the mirror showed an elegant woman.

A hairdresser from the hotel came to whip her newly grown locks into a confection on her head. A moment to fix the dainty diamond necklace about her neck, adjust a velvet wrap about her shoulders, a last check in the mirror, and it was time to go.

The car was there for her ten minutes early, and to make friendly conversation she congratulated the driver on his punctuality.

'Signor di Luca came looking for me and demanded to know why I hadn't gone yet,' he said with a grin. 'I told him I still have plenty of time, but he said, *go now!* So I did. It doesn't do to argue with the boss.'

'I gather he can be a real slave-driver,' she laughed.

'He's been worse recently. It's like the devil has got into him. Maybe it's because he had to waste time in hospital. He hated that.'

It might be no more than that, Alysa thought. But she couldn't help wondering if there might be something else. She would know when she saw him.

Elena was waiting for her on the step as the car drew up.

'How charming to see you again,' she said. 'Drago is detained for the moment, but he'll be down soon. Let me introduce you to Signorina

Leona Alecco. Our families have been friends for years.'

Leona was in her late thirties, slightly heavily built, not pretty, but with an intelligent face that would have been better with less make-up. Her neckline was just too low for her build, and made Alysa glad that she had opted for caution in her own dress.

The same idea might have occurred to Leona, for she gave Alysa a shrewd look, taking in every detail of her glamorous appearance before becoming carefully blank-faced.

'It's just a small gathering tonight,' Elena continued, ushering her inside. 'Only family and friends. Tomorrow we'll be inundated with businessmen and really important people.'

Just in case I delude myself that I'm important, Alysa thought wryly.

She took a glass of wine from the proffered tray and sipped it, looking around at the little gathering. Carlotta's sister was there again, with her husband and children. Leona seemed practically one of the family. She herself was the only outsider.

But not for long. Tina had spotted her and came

scurrying across the floor to seize her hands, beaming upwards as if Alysa was a dear friend.

'Poppa said you were coming,' she confided.

Alysa was touched. At their previous meeting she'd still been tormented by her own dead child, and had been unable to be at ease with the little girl. Yet Tina had seemed oblivious, offering her friendship then, and even more now. Alysa felt shamed by such open-hearted generosity. The smile she gave Tina was warm.

'Who's your friend?' she asked, indicating a doll in an elaborate dress that Tina was carrying.

'Aunt Leona gave it to me.'

'She's very pretty,' Alysa said politely, but Tina pulled a face.

'She's too *frilly*,' she complained. 'I don't like being frilly.'

'I know what you mean,' Alysa said at once. 'I've never been frilly myself. I used to prefer making mud pies.'

They nodded in perfect empathy.

A noise made her turn around to see Drago just coming into the room. The others seized on him at once, giving her a moment to look without being seen in return.

For the first time she saw him dressed formally in a dinner jacket and black bow-tie, whose elegance had the perverse effect of making him seem taller and more powerful than she remembered. Now she could perceive him as other women did—a deeply attractive man, made even more attractive by a touch of harshness—except that she had seen past that veneer and knew how thin it was.

At last Drago looked up and saw her, and a slow smile spread over his face. There was a look of satisfaction in his eyes, as though his best hopes had come true, but there was also an astonished question: *this is* her?

Seeing that surprised admiration, she knew she'd been secretly hoping for just this. The months apart vanished. He was the same man who had supported her and leaned on her at the same time, and when he came across the floor with his hands outstretched she reached out to him.

'I was afraid you wouldn't come,' he said softly.

'And miss your moment of glory?' she teased. 'Never.'

He didn't speak, but the pressure on her hands increased slightly.

'At last you're here,' Elena's voice broke in. 'I thought you'd never join us.'

Drago released Alysa and turned to smile politely at Elena.

'A potential client turned up without warning. I had to see him briefly, but I've put him off for a few days, so now we can have dinner. Shall we go in?'

'Of course. You're sitting next to Leona, and Tina is sitting next to me.'

'I want to sit next to Alysa,' Tina said at once, adding in a confiding voice, 'She's a guest.'

'And you are her hostess,' Drago said at once. 'So of course you must sit beside her and look after her for me.'

Elena looked displeased but was unable to protest. Tina took Alysa's hand and led her into the dining room, while Drago went unprotesting with Leona.

A suspicion was growing in Alysa's mind, which was increased as she saw Leona seated firmly on Drago's right. Elena regarded them both with the complacency of a match-maker who saw things working out.

She was deluding herself, Alysa thought. There was no sign of the lover in Drago's manner to

Leona. He was charming, considerate, but slightly detached. If Leona claimed his attention, he turned to her with a smile, but he seldom made the first move.

And yet, perhaps Elena knew what she was doing. Drago wasn't in love, but he wouldn't have been the first widower to marry a sensible woman to give his child a mother. An old family friend would be a logical choice, and help to keep Tina close to her grandmother.

But not this woman, Alysa mused. For reasons she couldn't explain, she wasn't sure that Leona was what he needed.

When the meal was under way, Tina confided, 'I wanted to ask you about Poppa. You did look after him, didn't you?'

'I think I did. I tried. He looked after me too.'

'Because you both had someone who died?'

'Yes, just so.'

By the time the meal ended, Tina's eyes were drooping, and Drago gently suggested that it was time for all the children to go to bed.

'Leona and I will take care of that,' Elena said at once. 'Come, children, upstairs.'

Alysa leaned down so that Tina could give her

a peck on the cheek. Then the child was whisked away by Elena.

'Come with me,' Drago said, taking Alysa's arm.

He led her out onto a terrace at the back of the house, overlooking the moonlit garden.

'Let me look at you,' he said.

He held her away from him, surveying her, while she did the same—both silently asking how their previous encounter had changed them. Alysa held her breath, wondering what he would say. At last he spoke.

'You've put on weight.'

'What?'

'Good. I like it. You were far too skinny before.'

Alysa burst out laughing. Trust him to say something no other man would have said.

'All right,' he said hastily. 'I'm not known for my tact.'

'You amaze me.'

'But I mean what I say. You were like a ghost before. Now you're alive again.'

'And what about you? Are you alive again?'

'In some ways, not in all. I have so much to tell you, my dear friend.'

'And I have things to tell you,' she said eagerly.

'You said I looked alive again, and I'm almost there, but there's still something I need badly and you're the only person who can help me.'

His eyes grew warmer and he seized her hands.

'But of course I'll help you—anything you ask. Who knows you better than I? Tell me now, what it is that you need?'

But before she could speak there was a call of, 'Drago,' and they looked back at the house to see Leona waving to him.

'Elena wants to talk to you,' she said.

'Will you be kind enough to tell her that I'll return in a moment?' he said.

'I think she wants you now. She says you're neglecting your guests.'

Drago groaned softly.

'You'd better go,' Alysa said.

'Yes, I suppose I must, but we must talk before you leave.'

He drew her hand through his arm and they went in together, Leona watching them like a hawk.

For the rest of the evening Alysa stayed in the background. Her moment would come later. At last she murmured to him, 'I should be going.'

'Fine, I'll drive you home,' Drago said.

Elena started to protest that that was the chauffeur's job, but Drago silenced her with a deadly smile.

'I know I can rely on you to be the perfect hostess while I'm gone. Alysa, are you ready?'

When they were on the road, safely away from the house, he said through gritted teeth, 'My mother-in-law!' Then, when Alysa gave a soft chuckle, 'Yes, I suppose you find it funny.'

'Well, she's so blatant about it. She's very determined to marry you to Leona, isn't she?'

'You saw that too? I hoped it was just my imagination.'

'It's obvious. She's like a general going into battle, with everything worked out.'

'How dreadfully true. When I invited her for tomorrow's ceremony, she somehow turned it into an invitation for Leona too.'

As they reached the outskirts of Florence, he said, 'Let's find somewhere to sit down and talk.'

He chose a small café in a side street and settled her in a corner where the light was poor and few people would notice them.

'Is that why you invited me here?' she asked. 'To protect you from Leona?'

'Not really, I just needed to see you. What happened seems so unreal. I wanted to be sure you really existed. But now you're here I'm glad, because of Leona too. I don't know what's got into Elena.'

'I suppose for her Leona would be the ideal choice because she wouldn't try to separate her from Tina as another woman might.'

'I gather they've got it all sorted. Don't I get a say in this arrangement?'

'Not much. After all, you might well decide to remarry for Tina's sake.'

'Never,' he said fiercely. 'Not just for Tina's sake, and not— Well, anyway.' He sighed. 'I don't want them choosing a wife for me. I rely on you to shield me from their intrigues.'

'Don't worry,' she assured him. 'I'm your best friend, and when the time comes I'll take a hand in choosing your wife. Tina and I will line up the candidates, put them through a series of tests and mark them one to ten.'

He laughed. 'Between you and her watching over me like a pair of guardian angels, I know I'll be safe. As for you being my best friend…'

'After all we went through together, don't you think I am?'

'I think—' He paused, as if undecided what to say next. 'I think we have a bond that will never be broken, and I want— Well, let's leave that for later. I only wish I could spend more time with you during the celebrations.'

'You have your duty to do, I know that.'

'But, afterwards, will you come to the mountains with me?'

Her heart leapt. 'I hoped you'd ask that.'

'But don't mention it to anyone else. As far as anyone knows, you're going back to England.'

'What do you take me for? I wasn't going to confide in Elena, was I?'

He grinned. 'No, I reckon you're a match for her. By the way, what was it you wanted to talk to me about?'

'It can wait. I'll tell you when we're in the mountains.'

'Now I'd better get back home, heaven help me. The car will come for you tomorrow.'

Next day a convoy drove the ten miles to the church, where it disgorged a seemingly endless line of distinguished Florentines. Drago escorted them around the building, describing everything that had been done, and received their congratulations with calm pleasure, not seeming to be overwhelmed by them.

He was his own man, Alysa thought. He knew he'd done a fine job, and he needed nobody else to tell him so.

Tina slipped away from her grandmother and attached herself to Alysa, explaining everything like an expert. Elena tried to draw her back to the family group, but the little girl had her father's stubbornness.

'I have to look after Alysa,' she explained firmly. 'She has nobody of her own.'

She clung to Alysa's hand until they were apart from the others.

'You see up there?' she said, pointing. 'That's where Poppa fell. He was terribly angry. He shouted at everyone.'

'Even you?'

'No, not me. Just everyone else. But he was better after you called. He told me about it.'

The ceremony was long and impressive. Several people rose to heap praise on Drago, which he received with a blank face that told her he was embarrassed.

Then it was time to return to the hotel so that she could prepare for the grand banquet that night. She had not managed to have a single word with Drago.

As she got into the car, Tina hugged her and asked anxiously, 'You will come tonight, won't you?'

Once the feel of those childish arms about her neck would have made her flinch. Now she hugged Tina back warmly.

'Promise,' she said.

In a sudden impulse she spent the afternoon shopping for a dress that was more daring than before, a soft-ivory chiffon that clung to her and emphasised her movements.

The villa was ablaze with lights as she joined the crowd streaming in later that evening. Drago stood there, greeting his guests with Elena on one side, and Leona on the other, as though her place in the villa was already assured. She greeted Alysa with lofty assurance, as did Elena, both women studying her attire suspiciously.

Drago studied it too, with a gleam in his eyes that won an answering smile.

Tina too was part of the reception line-up, but she slipped away to join Alysa, which won Drago's look of warm approval.

'Look what Poppa bought me,' she said, showing Alysa a locket around her neck. Inside was a picture of Carlotta.

'He said it was specially for today, because Mamma would have enjoyed this so much, and we must think of her.'

'Does he speak of her much?' Alysa asked.

'Oh yes, especially when it's her birthday— that was last week—and on my birthday, because she sends me presents. Well, it's Poppa really, but he says it's her, and I pretend to believe him 'cos otherwise he might be hurt.'

'And you don't want to hurt him, no matter what you have to do?'

Tina beamed at this understanding. 'He pretends to be a bully, but he isn't really. Just a big softy.'

'And nobody knows him better than you, so I guess you're right.'

'Tina!' It was Leona's voice. 'We are sitting down for dinner now. Come along.'

'But I've got lots of things to show Alysa.'

'Later,' Alysa said. 'Never keep your host waiting.'

'Very true,' Drago said from somewhere behind Leona, who turned to him.

As soon as her back was turned Tina seized the chance to stick her tongue out at her. Alysa hastily covered the child's mouth, but not before Drago saw and gave a wide grin.

It was all over in seconds, and then they were marching sedately to the banqueting hall. But it left Alysa feeling exhilarated. Leona might have been seated in the place of honour by Drago, but it was with her that he had the shared understanding.

She saw another side of him that night— assured and businesslike. He even managed to be charming, although she guessed he was carefully negotiating three moves ahead in such unfamiliar territory.

After dinner there was dancing to the accompaniment of an orchestra. Drago danced with Leona, then with a series of wives, mostly indistinguishable from each other, while Alysa entertained herself with several gentlemen who all spoke perfect English and had commercial interests in England. She could therefore assure herself, with a clear conscience, that she was touting for business.

She would have liked to dance with Drago. Something told her that it would be very interesting. But her time would come.

As the evening drew to a close Elena spoke to her from lofty heights.

'I hope you have really enjoyed your time here, *signorina*, and that you will return home with happy memories.'

Alysa made the polite response, and Elena immediately followed up with, 'When exactly do you leave?'

'I'll be going tomorrow.'

'How sad. We're going to stay here for a few more days. It's so seldom we can get the whole family together, and we simply must make the most of it.'

'I'm afraid the family gathering will be without me,' Drago put in. 'The man I told you about— the one who turned up last night—wants me to look over a building to see if it's worth renovating. I have to leave first thing tomorrow morning, and I'll be gone for several days.'

Elena began to protest, but his smile was implacable.

'Signora Dennis, let me escort you to the car,' he said. 'I only regret I am unable to drive you home myself.'

As she got into the waiting car, she said casually, 'I wonder where this building is?'

'You know quite well where it is,' Drago replied. 'Or have you forgotten what we agreed?'

'Not a word. I'll be waiting for you tomorrow. Now I'd better go quickly, before Elena does something desperate.'

CHAPTER TEN

'It's a pity you only saw the mountains under snow,' Drago said as they headed out of Florence next morning. 'I've wanted you to see them now, when everywhere is at its best.'

The journey was magical. Their last trip had been made in the chill of winter. Now they climbed higher into the sunlight, the trees glowing around them in the green of summer.

Again they stopped at the village to stock up on groceries, but slowly this time, while he asked her preferences and promised her a whole series of dishes to make her rejoice.

'Does this mean I can help with the cooking?' she asked as they got back into the car.

'Not at all. Stay out of my kitchen. A woman's place is laying the table.'

When they had driven on a little way, she said, 'Stop the car. I want to look.'

He pulled in just off the road, and they left the car behind to wander among the trees.

'You'd hardly know it was the same place,' Alysa said in wonder.

'Thank you for coming,' he said quietly. 'I've thought of you all the time. Say it was the same with you.'

'Oh yes. You were always with me.'

He took her hand and they wandered higher. The trees grew more luxuriantly here, blocking out much of the light so that the sunbeams slanted down like arrows piercing the shadows.

'Do you recognise this place?' he asked, stopping suddenly by a tree.

'I don't think so.'

'I guess you wouldn't. The last time you were here it was dark and snowing.'

'Is this where you found me that night?'

'That's right. You were curled up under this very tree.'

'I can hardly believe it. It's so beautiful now, and then it was—'

'Another world,' he said.

Leaning against the tree, he raised her hand so that he could brush the back of it against his cheek, hold it there for a moment, then press his lips against it.

'I've been back here often since you went away,' he said. 'It's where I come for peace, and even happiness.'

'Can there be happiness?' she asked wistfully.

'There might be.'

'It takes time.'

'Do you know the first lesson a builder has to learn?' he asked. 'Not to go too fast. Let things happen in their own time, or you'll make a mess of the whole project.'

'And we mustn't make a mess of the project,' she agreed.

His smile was fond and warm.

'Some projects are more important than others,' he said. 'Right, let's go. I'm getting hungry.'

She nodded at his abrupt change of tone. Having moved cautiously to the edge of the precipice, he'd backed off before asking her to look over. And he was right, of course, she thought as they hurried down to the car hand in hand. They had all the time in the world to find out what lay past the precipice.

The sun was setting on the little villa as they drew close, turning the roof to red. Drago parked his car in the garage where he'd once found her standing in the cold and lost his temper. Together they went upstairs to where a fire was already laid in the grate, waiting to be lit.

'Even in summer it gets a bit chilly when the light goes,' he said. 'So I came here a few days ago and got everything ready for you.'

Despite what he'd said, he allowed her to help with the meal that evening. They ate it in virtual silence, but it was silence with a special quality. She could see ahead now, just a little way, but it was enough for this evening. After that, who could tell?

This visit had already shown her that there was more to Drago than she had discovered last time, inspiring her with a passionate desire to explore him further—heart, mind and body.

When the meal was over, by mutual consent they settled down on the thick rug before the fire, leaning against each other.

'You're so different,' he said. 'You've flowered.'

'Yes, you told me I'd got fat, you cheeky so-and-so,' she murmured contentedly.

'I didn't say that and you know it. When we were here before you were on the same slippery slope that I was. Do you remember that day at the waterfall? If anyone had told me then what you would become to me I wouldn't have believed them.'

'Nor me. I just wanted to fight you, and then when you turned up at the airport and tricked me into coming up here—'

'I never tricked you.'

'May you be forgiven! That defeated air!'

'I was frightened. You were a very scary lady.'

'I scared myself sometimes. It scares me even more to look back at what I was becoming. I put you through it too, I remember—getting lost in the snow and you had to nurse me.'

'I didn't mind nursing you.'

'You did. You suddenly became very bad-tempered,' she remembered. 'You kept barking at me.'

'After finding you in that garage—'

'No, it was before that.'

'Oh yes, I remember.'

'What do you remember? Go on, tell me.'

He hesitated, then said wryly, 'All right, I'll

confess. When you got that heavy cold I was worried, so I stayed with you.'

'That's right.'

'I actually slept on the bed.'

'Outside the bedclothes, of course.'

'Of course!'

Alysa chuckled. 'How charming and old-fashioned. Positively nineteenth-century.'

'It's all very well to laugh, but you were ill, you were trapped with me, relying on me to look after you. Of course I was old-fashioned. At least, I meant to be, but I awoke to find that somehow I'd put my arm over you.'

She gasped. 'Shocking! How could you?'

'I was asleep, I didn't know—are you making fun of me?'

'Do you think I am?'

'I'm not sure,' he said cautiously. 'I don't have much sense of humour, but I think perhaps you are laughing.'

'It took you long enough to realise that,' she said gently, touched by the humility in his voice. 'Shall I promise not to laugh at you?'

'No, I don't mind if it's you. Make fun of me if you like. I might even come to understand.'

'Yes, I guess you might,' she said.

'It's just that I felt awkward next day, which is why I was a bit offhand. Anything was better than have you suspect. What is it?' Alysa had begun to laugh helplessly.

'You never guessed?' she crowed. 'Oh, I can't believe this.'

'What's so funny?'

'It was me. I slipped out to the bathroom, and when I came back you'd stretched your arm across the empty space. I eased myself in under it, being very careful not to disturb you, so that you didn't take it away.'

'You—?'

'I made it happen. It wasn't you, it was me.'

'But I felt so guilty because— And you let me suffer.'

'I didn't know you were suffering,' she chuckled. 'But I wish I had.'

'Yes, you'd have enjoyed it,' he said, chagrined. 'You—you—'

'Come on, you were going to develop a sense of humour.'

'I guess I'll need a little time for that. I can't take this in. I was feeling ashamed all that time and I didn't need to?' His tone was outraged.

'Something like that.'

'Well, I'll be—'

There was a light in his eyes that she was beginning to know. She'd seen it across the room on the night she'd arrived, and wanted to know more. Since then her curiosity had grown, and now she urgently needed to pursue it to the end. So when the words failed him, and he jerked her towards him with a grunt of frustration, she went into his arms willingly, and sighed with pleasure as his mouth touched hers.

It was he who was tentative, caressing her lightly with his lips, waiting for her response, then embracing her eagerly as he sensed the desire that she had no wish to hide. He'd been almost afraid of taking her by surprise, but now he knew that she'd been waiting for him, ready for this moment.

She was returning his kiss, her lips moving slowly but with determination, teasing and testing him, asking a question which he answered readily. Lightning seemed to streak through her. It was so long since she'd known the physical yearning for release that now it had the delight of the unexpected, as well as the pleasure of anticipation.

Now she knew that the flash of desire—so briefly sensed, so swiftly controlled, that she'd felt on the day months ago when he'd carried her home and their mouths had almost touched— had been no illusion. It had been both a promise and a warning: think carefully before going beyond this point.

She'd had months to think carefully, becoming more confused all the time. But suddenly everything was clear, and from now on there would be no more thinking.

Drago felt her reaching towards him, not just with her mouth but her whole being. He lacked the words to tell her how the hope of this moment had lured and tantalised him through the weary time apart, but movements, tender and urgent together, were saying everything for him.

Then he was laying her gently back against the thick carpet, opening her buttons, pulling her clothes away, dumbstruck as he discovered that she was already naked underneath. His astonishment delighted her, and she gave a slow smile that told him everything, relishing the dawning look of complicity in his eyes.

'You're a wicked woman,' he whispered.

'Have you only just learned that?'

'I never know what to think with you.'

'I could help you find out.'

After that nothing could have held him back. He touched her face with reverent fingers, then let them trail down her neck and onwards between her breasts while she lay trembling with the sensation, so sweet and so long-forgotten.

No, not forgotten: never known. James's love-making hadn't been like this. He'd known that she adored him and had accepted it as a right, never looking at her with the feeling bordering on awe that she saw now in Drago's eyes.

Her nights with James had been physically thrilling, but always with some element missing, because the emotion had been largely on her side. But Drago's heart was open to her own, filling her with joy, so that she lay back, her arms above her head, luxuriously spreading herself for his delight.

He moved his hands outwards, cupping her breasts in a gesture of tender possessiveness, then lay down so that his face was between them, his lips continuing the work of his fingers while she clasped her hands behind his head and arched up against him.

When he raised his head she began to open his shirt, and he helped her, moving feverishly, as though responding to a signal for which he'd been waiting too long.

When he too was naked, she had one moment of doubt. This was the first man for a year and a half. But, looking into his face, she saw the understanding that had never yet failed her.

'Me too,' he said softly. There was no need to say more.

His movements became more urgent. Request became demand. Plea shaded into insistence. His hands explored further, tracing a path on the inside of her thighs, until he reached the heart of her sensation and felt her tremble. In a moment he was over her, seeking, finding. Then he was inside, inviting her to enclose him.

She received him happily, knowing now that this was right in every way, feeling their bodies move together as though they had been made for each other. They were both so eager that their moment came quickly, almost taking them by surprise, before they had time to enjoy the pleasure to the full.

His skill and urgency were driving her on until she arched against him with a cry, and pulled him hard against her while his own release took hold of him. In the last seconds her movements were almost as wild as his own.

Afterwards she held him tightly, feeling him tremble, then grow calmer as the storm passed. He lay against her for a long time before raising himself to look down on her. He looked shaken.

'Are you all right?' he whispered.

'Mmm,' she murmured contentedly.

'I didn't mean to be so—so—'

He fell silent, so clearly embarrassed that she wanted to hug him. He was saying that he hadn't meant to be so fierce and nearly out of control. But that was what had pleased her most.

'It's just fine,' she assured him. 'I liked it that you were so—*so*—'

'You're on the floor, and it must be a bit hard.'

'Not with this lovely thick rug. Still, there are other places—more comfortable.'

He rose, drawing her with him, and they made

their way to his room, almost running in their eagerness to throw themselves onto the bed and revel in each other.

It was only a few minutes ago that they had made love, yet the desire was there again, eager and vibrant, so that they laughed with triumph and the joy of being alive and together. This time he cast aside restraint from the first moment, and she gave him a response that was almost violent in its lack of inhibition.

'What happened to the light?' she asked as they lay together afterwards. 'I don't remember it getting dark.'

'We were thinking of something else,' he said.

'I guess we were. Something much more important.'

'I wanted you so badly,' he murmured. 'But I was afraid in case I spoilt things.'

'I know,' she said lazily. 'We had something so good, I didn't want to risk it either. But I guess we couldn't stand still. Maybe this was always waiting for us.'

'How wise you are!'

He buried his face against her neck, relishing the scent of her.

'Sweetness and spice,' he murmured. 'Adventure and peace. How do you manage to be everything at once?'

'You're a poet!'

'Good grief, no!' he said, shocked. 'Oh, I see, you're laughing at me again.'

'Just a little,' she said tenderly. 'Don't worry about it.'

'I don't, not any more.'

They lay for a while, half-waking, half-dozing, until he said, 'Do you remember what I said when we parted at the airport, about being glad we hadn't met earlier?'

'Yes, I thought about it a lot, and in the end I knew you were right.'

'In the end?'

'I wasn't quite ready at first. I think I began to see it when you had that accident, and I was so afraid that you might be dead.'

'I was a bit ahead of you. I felt so close to you that it scared me. The first time I came back to this place, I left at once; it was so empty without you. I meant never to return, but then I found I had to write to you, just to keep some sort of contact. When you replied I came up here again. And you were here too. You've been here ever since.'

'I know,' she said. 'I always knew I was in this place with you.'

'Did you suffer much when you returned home?'

'At first, yes. I cried a lot, but even then I knew that it was good to cry. Everything had been trapped inside me for a year, and it was destroying me. Very soon it would have been too late. When I stopped crying I knew that I'd come through it, and since then I've got stronger. The world doesn't frighten me any more.'

'I don't believe the world ever frightened you,' he said wryly. 'More like the other way around.'

'That was just the surface. I kept my armour in place to hide my fear. I don't have to do that any more. What about you? Has anything been better?'

'I haven't your courage. I still feel easier wearing the armour, except with you. But, like I told you, I sleep better. Tina is happier.'

In the poor light she could just make out the scar on his forehead, and she reached up to touch it.

'Is that where you got hit?'

'Yes, it's fading now.'

'I thought you were dead. Everything went

dark. The thought of you not being there any more—even if I didn't see you, I knew you were there, and if suddenly you weren't—I didn't know how I'd manage without you.'

'I can remember lying in the hospital and thinking about you, wishing you were with me. And then you called. I think that was when I began plotting to get you out here again. I had to see you, to reassure myself that it hadn't been a dream.'

'Well, I'm here now, but it does feel like dreaming. I don't know what's real any more. Was this always going to happen?'

'Don't you know the answer to that?' he asked seriously.

The question pulled her up short. Hadn't she always known that they would end up embracing, exploring each other on the only level they hadn't yet discovered?

'I guess, if you'd just let me go home, I wouldn't have liked it. I wouldn't have liked it at all. It would have meant that something had gone wrong.'

'Me too. And I wasn't going to let it go wrong.'

'So you had this planned from the first moment?'

'Not planned. Hoped. I didn't know how it was

going to work out until the other night at the villa, when I looked up and saw you standing there—so beautiful, so changed in the way I'd been hoping for. And then I knew.'

'Yes,' she said, remembering the moment when she'd seen him again, the king in his own domain. 'That was when I knew too.'

'Hmm,' he said, leaning his head on her.

'Hey, you're nearly asleep.'

'No, not really.'

'Just the same,' she said with a little chuckle, 'you are. So I may as well join you. Goodnight.'

At breakfast he said, 'I thought today we'd go out, and I'll show you how lovely this place can be. Then we'll eat in a tiny restaurant in the village.'

'Wouldn't it be nicer to eat here? Just the two of us?'

'You're right. We'll come straight back.'

The walk up the mountain was magic. As they climbed the gentle slope the sun glinted through the trees, so that they passed from shadow to sunlight to shadow again. Now and then he would take her into his arms and they would stand locked together in silence.

It seemed that there was nobody else for miles, as though they were alone in all the world, with nothing to think of but each other. When there was a gap in the trees they stood looking up at the birds flying overhead, transfixed by the beauty.

'I love you,' he said.

Alysa turned her head slowly, wondering if she'd imagined it. He looked back at her, answering her thought.

'Yes, I love you. Why do you look surprised? You shouldn't be.'

'I suppose you're right,' she said, dazed.

'You said you could see where we were heading,' he reminded her.

'Yes, but—I guess I only saw a little way ahead.'

As she said it she couldn't help smiling as she thought of their time in bed.

'I know,' he said. 'There was a time when I too only saw that much. But it's not enough. Without love it's nothing.'

'But you're going too fast for me. I think I've lost faith.'

'In me?' he asked quietly.

'No, in me. Love costs so much, and I can't pay

that price any more. I guess that makes me a coward.'

'You? Not in a million years.'

'Yes, me. When I think of how I loved before, throwing myself into it heedlessly, I know I can't be like that again.'

'Of course not. No two loves are the same any more than people are the same. I love you differently from Carlotta, but not less. Or is this your way of saying that I'm fooling myself and you don't love me?'

She took so long answering that his brow darkened. 'Is it that?'

'I don't know. How can I tell? You're dearer to me than anyone else on earth, but— How can I explain? Part of me doesn't want you to be.'

'So you're going to fight me until you've driven me out? I'm stubborn, Alysa. I won't go easily. I'll haunt your mind and heart until you turn to face me. Night and day I'll be with you every moment.'

'Yes—yes,' she whispered.

'Stay with me. Marry me. Love me.'

'You make it sound so easy,' she said with a touch of anger. 'It isn't. Love's more dangerous than you know.'

'You really believe I haven't learned that?'

'You think you have, but you don't know—'

She stopped, horrified at what she'd nearly revealed. She'd been on the verge of telling him about the letter, the one thing she must never do. Too late she saw the trap she'd laid for herself.

'What don't I know?' he asked, looking at her keenly.

'You don't know anything,' she improvised hastily. 'We think we know, but we never really do.'

'What don't I know, Alysa?'

'Stop pressurising me,' she flashed. 'I only meant that nothing is how we think it is, and that's why nobody ever learns from experience. They never recognise the experience when it comes around the second time.'

He was giving her a curious look.

'I wonder what you really meant to say,' he mused. 'You're doing what my daughter calls talking "itty-bitty". It means floundering for words just to change the subject.'

'It's only that we're going too fast,' she pleaded.

'How can you say that after last night? We made love.' He eyed her uncertainly. 'Didn't we?'

'I don't know what we did. It was beautiful, but—'

'Yes, it was beautiful. You're not trying to say that it was only sex, are you?'

'No, but—'

'We've wanted each other. Don't tell me it was all on my side. Not after the way you came to life in my arms, and the things you whispered to me.'

'I've wanted you as well, but it doesn't have to be love. I won't go through that again.'

'Alysa, listen,' he said seriously. 'I don't want to love you any more than you want to love me. Do you think I haven't fought this? I have, day and night. But we may have no choice.'

'We're free beings. We make our own choices.'

'Nobody is as free as that. I thought I'd always be hounded by Carlotta, and everything that happened. But *you* set me free. Now it's you that I need.'

'Drago, please, don't rush me.'

'You mean I should stand back while you return to that life you've made a refuge because you think it's safer than love?' His voice became grimly ironic. 'A partnership in a firm of accountants! How can I compete with that?'

'You're not being fair.'

'Maybe not, but that's another thing about love—it isn't fair. Or is there something else that you're hiding?'

'Stop trying to steamroller me,' she cried. 'Give me a chance to think.'

'I didn't mean—' He checked himself with a groan. 'I'm doing it again, aren't I? Coming on strong, trying to pressurise you.'

'Does it work well with business negotiations?' she asked wryly.

He nodded. 'I've bullied people before,' he sighed. 'But I should have remembered that it doesn't work with you.'

'No, I bully back too well,' she said, trying to lighten the atmosphere. 'Why don't we go back now?'

CHAPTER ELEVEN

As THEY walked back to the villa Drago smiled and talked pleasantly, but Alysa felt with a heavy heart that the sun had gone in for them. He was no longer at ease with her, and she couldn't blame him. She wasn't at ease with herself. She didn't even begin to understand herself.

She had thought of him ceaselessly, had felt close enough to be his other self, despite the miles apart. Yet when the moment had come she'd backed off, driven away from him by a force too strong for her to resist.

Am I crazy? she thought. *Or just reasonable? We've only spent a little time together. It's an illusion that we know each other—a beautiful illusion, but the risk is too great. Why can't I take risks any more?*

As they were drinking wine after dinner that

evening, Drago said, 'The day you arrived you said there was something you wanted to say to me. We never did get round to discussing that.'

For a moment she couldn't think what he meant. The events of the last few days had blotted out everything but him. Then it came back to her.

'Oh yes. Something happened that day—I suddenly knew what I want to do most. If only I could make you understand…'

'Try me,' he said gently.

She was too distracted to look at him closely, or she might have seen the renewed hope in his eyes.

'It's about James,' she said. 'I want to make my peace with him.'

He frowned and drew back a little. 'But how can you do that?'

'I went to the cemetery again. He looked so lonely among the rejects, and I was the person who put him there.'

'Nonsense. He put himself there.'

'In a sense, yes, but when I denied all knowledge of him just after he died I banished him. Now I'd like to take him home.'

His head shot up. *'What?'*

'I want to have him returned to England and buried there. It's terrible to see him in that corner when Carlotta is still honoured. At least he should have a little kindness. What are you staring at?'

'I think you must have taken leave of your senses.'

The light had died out of his eyes and a kind of ferocity had taken its place.

'After all this time,' he said, 'everything that's happened—you still haven't freed yourself from him. Have you learned nothing?'

'Yes, I've learned that I have to forgive him before I can find peace.'

'You don't owe him anything.'

'You don't owe Carlotta anything, but you still cover her with flowers. I know it's partly for Tina, but there's more to it. You've forgiven her, and this is my way of forgiving James. But I need you to help me.'

'How?'

'You know people, you can use your influence to get me the necessary permissions.'

'Not in a million years,' he said flatly.

'But why?'

'Have you any idea what you're asking? Do

you think it's easy to raise a coffin and send it to another country? I thought you'd got beyond this point and put him behind you,' he said angrily.

'He *is* behind me.'

'I don't think so. Not if you'll go to all this trouble to keep him with you.'

'It's not like that.'

'Isn't it? Are you sure?'

She could see that he was really angry, and disappointment swept her. She'd been so certain she could rely on him, and now he was letting her down. Something stubborn rose within her. If that was how it was, she wouldn't beg.

'Fine. I'll manage this on my own. That's what I should have done from the start.'

'Then maybe that's it—the thing that was keeping you away from me. The truth is you still love him.'

'No! I don't love him, but I'm still not free of him, any more than you're free of Carlotta.'

'Don't try to pretend it's the same thing,' he growled. 'We were married for ten years. She gave me the child I love. She was a good wife, except for the end.'

He was looking at her with hard, challenging

eyes. Remembering what she knew, Alysa felt her temper flare.

'That's just it,' she raged. 'She was "a good wife" because she had a family who wanted to think of her that way, but James had no family, nobody to defend him except me.'

'He rejected you.'

'And *she* rejected *you*, but you haven't faced it. That's why her grave is still covered in red roses, because you have to cling to your image of her.'

'Then how come I told you I love *you*?' he shouted.

'Maybe you do, but I'm second best, and I always will be as long as you have this fantasy picture of her as the perfect wife—except for the fact that she left you.'

'Suppose I do think of her like that. Give me one good reason why I shouldn't.'

The challenge took her breath away. She could do exactly what he suggested, if only he knew. One sight of that letter and his illusions would vanish. For a moment she hovered on the verge of temptation.

'Well?' Drago persisted. 'You think you know her better than I did. Why don't you tell me why?'

Alysa let out her breath slowly.

'I'm not saying that. All I know of her is what happened at the end.'

'You mean when she took James from you. I understand why you hate her, but don't expect me to hate her as well.'

The air seemed to be singing in her ears. She had only to tell him the brutal truth, and back it up by fetching the letter from its hiding place in England. It would be so easy to do.

'No,' she said at last with a sigh. 'It wouldn't be right to hate her.'

The moment had passed. She wouldn't tell him now.

His phone rang. It was Tina. Alysa went into the kitchen and began washing up. She was just finishing when he came in.

'Tina seems to be finding Elena rather hard-going,' he said.

'Then you should get back to her as soon as possible,' Alysa advised at once. 'She comes first. And I have to be going home.'

'Ah yes, Brian and the partnership. I'm surprised he could let you go.'

'I told him I was touting for business.' With a

little laugh she showed she wasn't troubled. 'In a sense it was true. There were a lot of amazing people in your house, some with business interests in England, so I may do very well out of this visit.'

'I'm glad it wasn't a complete waste,' he said stiffly.

'Nothing's ever wasted with me. I can always turn things to good account.'

He took a step forward and seized her shoulders.

'*Stop it!* Don't talk like that. Who do you think you're dealing with?'

'I'm trying to make this easier for both of us.'

'Like hell you are. You're turning yourself back into *her*, aren't you?'

She didn't need to ask who he meant by 'her': that other self who'd lived behind a wall of ice, and who might still tempt her when things became painful.

'I'm being sensible. You have to leave, I have to leave,' she said. 'Would you rather I threw a hissy fit and begged you to put me first and your little girl second? That would be selfish and disgusting, and you know it.'

He groaned, running his hand through his hair.

'Yes, it would. But it worries me when you talk of being sensible. It's dangerous.'

'It's my natural state,' she said in a rallying tone.

'In that case, let's be sensible, and get ready to leave early tomorrow,' he said, scowling.

'Fine. I'll get packed.'

Suddenly she was glad to be leaving. The hope that had vibrated so thrillingly between them was dead, and there was no reason to stay.

Nothing was said, but they both knew they would sleep apart that night, and after their meal they retired to different rooms. Now she was in the same room where she'd slept when she'd first come here, listening for sounds coming from next door. But there was nothing, only silence, like the silence between them.

Next day he drove her to the airport.

How different this was from last time, she thought sadly. Then the atmosphere between them had been charged with hopes unfulfilled and hopes for the future that might yet be fulfilled. Their parting had been yearning and bittersweet. Now it was only resigned and slightly despairing.

At the barrier they paused and regarded each other.

'I guess we only managed to get part-way down the road,' he told her.

'We asked for too much,' she said sadly.

'I don't believe it was too much. I told you that I love you. That won't change. When you've decided what you want, I'll still be here.'

'You'd better forget about me. My head's too mixed up.'

'And so is your heart,' he said. 'But when you're ready to move on you'll find me here, however long it takes. When you come back— No, don't shake your head. You will come back.'

'Because that's what you've decided?' she asked with a faint smile.

'If you want to put it that way. I won't take no for an answer. I'm a tyrant, remember? An awkward, overbearing lout who demands his own way in everything.'

Her eyes were suddenly misty as she reached out to touch his cheek. He might bad-mouth himself as much as he liked, this great, gentle man with the tender eyes and the fierce armour that kept slipping, leaving him defenceless. She knew the truth, and her heart broke because she couldn't cast aside caution and throw herself into his arms for ever.

'No, that's not what you are,' she said. 'Tina was right.'

'What did Tina say about me?'

'Ask her. If you play your cards right, she might tell you.'

'If you're playing mind games with me,' he said, 'then we're not finished.'

He held her eyes with his own.

'I'll see you,' he said. 'I don't know when, but I will.'

Then he walked away.

Alysa landed in England at midday and behaved like a perfect, responsible business-woman, going straight into work and conferring with her colleagues. After four hours she departed with an arm full of files and spent the evening on the phone to clients.

Finally, at one in the morning, she faced the thing she'd been avoiding, and unlocked the safe where she kept Carlotta's letter.

She read it through once more, thinking of how

it would destroy Drago's illusions if he saw it, castigating herself as a fool who didn't know where her own best interests lay.

Tell him, urged her common sense. *It'll hurt him for a while, but it'll clear the way for you. You'll have all his heart then, and perhaps that will conquer your fear and free you to turn to him.*

But she knew she wasn't going to do it. It wasn't about common sense. It was about the love she felt even while she tried to deny it. It scared her that she'd come so close to telling him the forbidden secret.

She took out the letter from James that she'd also stolen, and read them both one last time. Then she tore them into little pieces, put a match to them and watched as they turned to ashes.

As the months passed she found herself doing again what she'd done before, throwing herself into the job to dull emotions that she didn't want to have. But it was harder now. Then she hadn't fully understood what she was doing. This time she knew exactly.

She'd survived once by murdering all feeling and functioning like an automaton, but Drago had destroyed that defence. Now her heart was alive again, and it yearned for him. He'd shown her a new way, and she'd rejected it.

But I can't face it going wrong again, she mourned. *Not just for me, but for him. This is my life now.*

As the time passed into November, then December, the weather grew cold—not the bright, edgy cold of approaching Christmas, but a dreary chill. Decorations went up in the office; lists were made of clients who must be sent cards.

More as a personal gesture than anything, Alysa put a few modest decorations up in her home. It wasn't the joyful display of the Christmas before last, when she'd been full of ill-fated happiness over James. But nor was it the bleak nothingness of last year, when she'd hurried past shop windows containing nativity scenes, eyes averted. She'd come to terms with what her life was turning into. Or so she told herself.

If she'd felt like weakening fate took a hand just then to stiffen her resolve, Brian chose that moment to tell her that her partnership was settled.

'We're going to make an occasion of it,' he said.

'Dinner at the Ritz, with everyone there—all the partners and their wives—just to welcome you. I'll be your escort, so take tomorrow off to buy a new dress. Go on. I don't want to see you in the office until you've bought something eye-catching.'

Next morning she got up early to head for the West End, but she soon realised that it was going to be one of those awkward days. As she was heading for the lift, she heard the phone begin to ring in her apartment, dashed back, dropped her keys and managed to get the front door open just as the ringing stopped.

She punched in the keys to find out where the call had come from, but there was nothing to tell her.

Which means it's probably a foreign number, she thought. *Drago?*

It wasn't wise to call him, but she found herself dialling his number. But all she got was the engaged signal. She held on, hoping it would stop. When it didn't she hung up and dialled again. Still engaged.

Not Drago, then. Probably a wrong number.

But it happened again, just as she reached the front door. This time she ran back fast, but the ringing stopped just as she reached out her hand.

'Well, you're not Drago,' she told the phone when she'd slammed it down. 'He'd never dither like that. Now, I'm going.'

The streets were full of Christmas. Neon angels floated overhead, their lights flickering on and off even at this early hour. Music played, notices announced, 'this way to Santa Claus'. Alysa entered one of London's exclusive department-stores and found herself almost caught up in the queue for Santa.

She could see him in the distance, sitting at the entrance to his grotto, talking earnestly with a little boy, apparently asking what he wanted for Christmas.

The impossible question, Alysa thought. *Two years ago I'd have said that I already had every-thing I could want—James and our baby. Last year I'd have said I was all right then, that I'd put the past behind me, never dreaming that Drago lay in the future.*

But what would I say now—that a few weeks ago I stood at a crossroads and made the wrong choice? That it's too late to go back? That my future is now my past, and my heart aches for the love I wasn't brave enough to fight for?

While she mused her feet took her to the entrance to the fashion department, and she forced herself back to the present. Her big moment had come and she was here to celebrate. She repeated that to herself again and again, hoping that it would become real. Or would, at least, start to matter.

The dress she finally chose was dark red, dramatic and magnificent, hugging her waist and hips, and low-cut—just the right side of decency. To go with it she chose a pair of golden sandals with suicidally high heels. The whole outfit was unlike anything she'd worn before, and that was fine. This was her flag of triumph.

On her return to the office she was besieged by her secretary and two others, demanding a display, so she dressed up and paraded before them. For this she'd sacrificed everything, and she was going to enjoy it. Their cries of delight attracted the others in the office. Brian appeared, adding his admiration, and soon everyone was applauding as she paraded up and down. They all knew that she was the victor about to come into her kingdom.

'Make way for the queen!' one of them cried.

'Is this vision the lady I'm to have the honour of escorting?' Brian asked.

Laughing, she turned to him and curtseyed, which made everyone cheer.

But the cheering died abruptly into silence. And Alysa turned to find Drago standing there, watching her, tension in every line of his body.

He looked as if he hadn't slept for a week. His eyes were haggard and desperate, and he reminded her of the man she'd first seen months ago at the waterfall. He carried the same aura that he'd had then, as though he was being devoured inside.

'I must speak with you,' he said harshly. 'Now.'

He looked around at the others, silently ordering them away. They were inclined to protest at this high-handedness, but Alysa said, 'Please leave us.'

They trickled away. Brian regarded her with raised eyebrows, but at last he too departed. As soon as they were alone she went to Drago.

'What's happened? Whatever is the matter?'

'I've come because I must take you back with me. It's vital.'

'But why? I can't leave now—'

'You *must*! No—no, I don't mean that. But I

can't tell you how important it is. Help me, Alysa, I beg you. You're the only person who can.'

'What's happened?'

'I was going to call you,' he said distractedly. 'But when I picked the phone up I knew I couldn't say it like that.'

'Drago, was that you on the phone this morning?'

'Yes, I called, then lost my nerve and hung up. Then I did it again.'

'But I thought it was you, and I called you back. It was engaged.'

'I was sitting there with the receiver in my hand, trying to make up my mind. Just an indecisive idiot. You'd have laughed if you'd seen me.'

'No, I wouldn't,' she said gently. 'Drago, please try to tell me what's happened. I've never seen you in such a state.'

He closed his eyes.

'Tina knows,' he said simply.

'What?'

'She knows that Carlotta had left for good. She knows her mother abandoned her.'

'But how?'

'She found out at school. One of the teachers

is a client of Carlotta's law firm, and of course the people there know the truth and talk about it. Tina overheard the teachers saying how Carlotta had just walked out on her, without caring if she never saw her again.'

He broke into a stream of curses. Alysa listened in horror, not following the words, but understanding the meaning, which perfectly expressed the violence of her own feelings.

'Oh God!' she whispered. 'What happened?'

'Tina came home sobbing her heart out. I've tried to comfort her, told her it's a misunderstanding, that her mother would never leave her.'

'Good, you stick to that,' Alysa said robustly. 'Is Elena any help?'

'She's denying it too, which helps a little, but she blames me for everything.'

'But how can it be your fault if people gossip in the law firm?'

'It can't, but Elena's seen her chance to get Tina away from me. She says I must have told her. I've denied it over and over, but she just calls me a liar. She says I'm a wicked influence, and she's going to "save" Tina from me. She wants to take her for good.'

'You mustn't let her,' Alysa said at once.

'I don't mean to, but I can't fight her alone. I told you about her family with its grand connections. It also contains two lawyers and a politician, and their influence is immense. They might just manage it.'

'But don't you have a lot of influence too?'

'Yes, I can afford good lawyers. But Elena can present herself so well, and I present badly, especially if I lose my temper. You're the only one who can help me,' he said. 'Tina likes you, and you can talk to her—explain, comfort her.'

'But explain what? What do you want me to say?'

'That's up to you. Whatever it is you'll manage better than me. I love that little girl, but I don't know what to say. I've tried and tried, but my words don't comfort her. She needs something more. You can give her that something, and make all those people see that they mustn't take her away from me.

'Please, Alysa, come back with me now. Tina and I need you more than you'll ever know.'

'Come back?' she echoed.

'There's a flight in three hours. We can just

catch it if we hurry. I promised Tina I'd be home tonight.'

'You've left her alone?'

'No, of course not. She's with a friend of mine and his wife. She knows them, and they can be trusted, but I have to return when I promised. Please, Alysa.'

She looked down at herself. Drago did the same, and for the first time he seemed to become aware of what she was wearing.

'What did I interrupt?' he asked.

'I just bought this for a dinner party.'

'And wore it in the office to show off to your escort. He's the guy I saw you with before, isn't he?'

'Yes,' came Brian's voice from the door. 'And the party is to celebrate her partnership.'

'Congratulations,' Drago said heavily. 'You got what you wanted.'

'Drago—'

'All I ask is that you help me out in this matter, and then I'll never trouble you again.' He lowered his voice. 'Please, Alysa, just come with me tonight.'

'Come where?' Brian asked.

'Florence,' Alysa said.

'Florence, Italy?' Brian sounded aghast.

'It would only be for a day,' Alysa pleaded. 'I'd rush back.'

'Alysa, this is Wednesday. The dinner is on Friday. You can't be sure you'll be back in time, and if you're not there when I've laid it all on…' He left the implication hanging in the air.

'I will be, I promise.'

'And what about tomorrow? Don't you have appointments?'

'My secretary will reschedule them. It'll be all right, but I have to go.'

'I'm surprised at you, Alysa,' Brian said. 'You've worked hard for this. I watched you with admiration, and I can't believe that you'd risk everything at the last minute.'

'You mean you'd take it all away from her because she missed one dinner party?' Drago demanded.

'We prefer our partners to be reliable,' Brian explained. 'And,' he added with a significant glance at Alysa, 'I'd rather not be made to look foolish. Don't disappoint me at this late date.'

'I won't. I'll be back, I swear it. But I must go, Brian.'

Brian looked at her for a moment, then gave a shrug that clearly meant, 'on your own head be it', and disappeared.

'Give me a moment to get changed,' Alysa said.

She did it in double-quick time, instructed her secretary, then hurried out with Drago. They didn't speak on the short journey to her home. She was trying to take in the enormity of what she'd done, aware of Drago watching her with a slightly baffled expression, as though he too had been taken by surprise.

They kept the taxi while she packed hurriedly, and then they were on their way to the airport.

'Suppose I can't get a ticket for this flight?' she asked.

'I took the liberty of buying you one.'

'Why didn't I think of that?' she asked with a little smile.

'Yes, you might have expected it by now. Will he really make you suffer for this?'

'I'll be back by Friday evening, so he'll have nothing to complain about. Don't worry.'

She wished she felt as confident as she sounded,

but she could see the threat looming before her. Elena's takeover bid for Tina had assumed manic proportions. She'd thought to control Drago by marrying him off to her friend, but that had failed, and now she was clutching at straws.

The idea that she could steal the little girl from her father might sound paranoid, but that didn't mean it shouldn't be taken seriously. Alysa pitied the old woman's suffering, but she wasn't going to see Drago devastated. Only she really understood what he'd lost, and while she had breath in her body he wasn't going to lose any more.

And if that meant that she was the loser, that she'd pay the price by throwing away everything she'd worked for, what then?

She glanced at Drago in the corner of the taxi, his eyes closed, light and darkness chasing each other across his face, and she reached out to touch him. At once he gripped her hand painfully tight. She returned it just as hard, and they sat like that for the rest of the journey.

CHAPTER TWELVE

DRAGO hardly spoke on the plane, and Alysa didn't offer words of consolation that would have been useless. His face was drawn and haggard. Sometimes he made the effort to smile at her, but she could see the truth beneath it. He was in a hell of fear. She smiled back, telling him she was there for him.

It was snowing at the airport, where his car was waiting to take them to the home of the friends who were caring for Tina. Florence itself was bright and cheerful, the streets full of decorations, the lights gleaming against the darkness of the sky and the white of the snow.

'We'll be there in a minute,' Drago said at last. 'It's getting late. She'll think I'm not coming—'

'Stop it,' Alysa said firmly. 'It's going to be all right. When you see her you'll smile, she'll throw herself into your arms and we'll take it from there.'

But she spoke with more confidence than she felt. Elena wasn't going to see her best chance slip away without a fight, and as the house came into view she sensed that her worst fears were being realised. All the lights were on, the front door was open, and a woman was standing outside looking frantically along the road.

'That's Signora Lenotti,' Drago said. 'I left Tina with her and her husband.' As the car stopped he leapt out. 'It's all right, we're here.'

But the woman burst into tears at the sight of him.

'What's happened?' Drago demanded.

'The *signora* was here. She demanded that I hand Tina over to her.'

'But you didn't,' Drago snapped. 'Tell me that you didn't.'

'What else could I do?' Maria wailed. 'She said she was her legal guardian, and she threatened me with the law.'

Drago swore violently.

'She just marched in and walked through the house,' Maria said. 'When she found Tina she— she acted as though we'd kidnapped her, telling her everything would be all right now that she'd been "rescued".'

'That poor little mite,' Alysa said. 'What must she be imagining now?'

'How did she even know she was here?' Drago raged.

'I think someone in your house told her,' Maria said.

'I gave them strict instructions not to.'

'But are they all loyal to you?' Alysa put in. 'I'll bet she's got at least one of them on her side.'

'My God, she'll stop at nothing,' Drago muttered. 'I never knew until this moment what I was dealing with.'

'Where does Elena live?' Alysa asked. 'We've got to go on there.'

'She's in Bologna,' Drago said. 'That's about sixty kilometres north of here.'

'Then let's go.'

It was dark and the road was winding, but Drago's driver was the best, and he had them there in an hour, finally drawing up outside a splendid villa.

'There are no lights on,' Alysa said, fearing the worst. 'But why? They must be expecting you.

Maybe they've just gone to bed,' she said, but she guessed they were both clutching at straws.

She knew the worst a moment later when the housekeeper came to the door and declared that the mistress had been away for two days, and she didn't know where she was or when she was coming back.

'My God, she could have taken Tina anywhere,' Drago groaned.

'Her other daughter,' Alysa said. 'Where does she live?'

'No, that family is in America at the moment, attending a wedding.'

'What about Leona? Where does she live?'

'Florence,' he said desperately.

'Fine. Let's get going.'

The driver had the engine running as they approached the car, and in a moment they were heading back the way they had come.

All the time Alysa was praying that Leona's house would be the end of the journey, and that this wouldn't turn into a hideous search for a child who'd completely disappeared.

When at last they saw the house she was fearful, for again the lights were off. But it was

Leona herself who came to the door, and Alysa could see at once that she was uncomfortable.

'Is my daughter here?' Drago demanded.

She nodded and stood aside to let him in, looking anxiously at his face.

'Elena just turned up here without warning,' she said in a placating voice. 'She had Tina with her—'

'And so you couldn't turn them away,' Alysa said at once. 'You had to keep Tina safe until her father came for her. That was very kind.'

Leona smiled at this understanding and hurried away.

'Why are you sympathising with her?' Drago demanded, outraged.

'Because it's not her fault, and she hates the situation,' Alysa said hurriedly. 'Don't you see? She's already half on your side. Let's keep her there and get her the rest of the way. If you come on strong you'll alienate her and this will be harder.'

When he hesitated, unconvinced, she said, 'Drago, why did you bring me here? Because you knew I could deal with this better than you can. So let me get on with it and don't interfere.'

After a moment he nodded, and she saw something she recognised. He had the same weary, defeated look that she'd seen at the airport in February. He was out of his depth, and he knew it.

'Thank you,' he whispered.

She touched his face and turned back to the stairs, where Leona had just appeared at the top of it.

'I've knocked on her door but she won't come out,' she said frantically. 'She's locked it on the inside.'

'Where's Tina?' Alysa asked.

'In there with her.'

Beside her Alysa felt Drago stiffen, about to launch a thunderbolt, but her grip on his hand stayed him.

'Please take me up to them,' she said.

They went up the stairs, along a corridor, with Drago determinedly following them, but keeping a cautious distance. At last they stopped outside a door. Alysa tried it but it didn't give. From inside she could hear the sound of Elena sobbing.

'Hello?' she called.

'Go away,' Elena screamed.

'Elena, please let me in.'

'Go away! You tell lies, all of you. I won't let you lie about her.'

'Tina,' Alysa said. 'Are you there? It's Alysa.'

Then came Tina's voice by the door. 'I'm here.'

'Can you open the door for me?'

A pause, then a click as the bolt was shot back. But then there was a scream of, *'No!'* from inside, and the sound of a scuffle. As Alysa entered she saw that Elena had managed to seize Tina and drag her to the other side of the room. Now she was sitting on the bed with the little girl in her arms.

For a moment Alysa felt a spurt of temper. How dared this woman subject a child to such pressure? But then she saw Elena's face streaming with tears, her eyes crazed with misery, her chest heaving with sobs.

Through finding each other, she and Drago had come to terms with their own grief, but Elena's loss could never be healed in the same way. She knew it, and the knowledge had driven her to desperation.

'You're all liars,' Elena choked. 'You say wicked things about my daughter, but they're not true, *they're not true.*'

Alysa had a split second to make her decision, or rather to recognise that the decision had already been made. As the words came out of her mouth, she knew that she could have said nothing else.

'No, they're not true,' she said. 'But nobody has been telling lies. It's a simple misunderstanding, and I'm here to put it right.'

She reached out to Tina, but Elena tightened her arms and drew the child away towards the head of the bed.

'Don't come any nearer,' she said hoarsely.

'Just this far,' Alysa said, and sat down on the bed, close enough to Tina to reach out for her hand and feel the little girl grip her hard.

'They said Mamma wasn't coming back,' she whispered. 'They said she didn't love me any more, and she just left me.'

'That is nonsense,' Alysa said firmly. 'Listen, darling, I'm going to tell you something. I met your mother on the day she died, at the waterfall. I'd gone there with James, a friend, meaning to go up in one of those chairs. While we were waiting for the next ride we went to a little coffee shop nearby. Your mamma was there, also waiting, and we started to chat.

'She told us about her husband and her little girl, and how she was looking forward to getting back to them. She'd been away on business, and her route back lay past the waterfall, so she'd stopped off for a ride because she loved the excitement. "Then I'm going home to my darlings", she said.'

Tina's gaze was fixed on her. Alysa drew a long breath, knowing that she must tell the next bit carefully.

'I enjoyed listening to her,' she said. 'Because I was in love, and I wanted to get married and have children that I would love as much as she loved you. She made it sound so wonderful.'

'Truly?' Tina whispered.

'Truly. She loved you more than anyone in the world.'

'What about Poppa?'

'Yes, she loved him too, but you most of all.'

'And she wasn't going to leave me?'

'No, she wasn't, or she couldn't have spoken as she did that day. She was full of plans about all the things you were going to do together.'

Vaguely she was aware that Elena had grown still. Her grip on Tina had relaxed, and her gaze was fixed on Alysa as if she too was hanging on every word.

'Then we walked out to the waterfall,' Alysa went on, 'to get into the rides, but at the last minute I lost my nerve and stayed on the ground. I never had much head for heights. It was really James who wanted to go.'

Somewhere behind her she heard Drago draw in a sharp breath, but she couldn't let herself be distracted now.

'Was James your friend who died?' Tina asked softly.

'Yes. I backed out at the last minute, so he and your mother went up together, and then— Well, they died together. He was the man in the chair with her. That's why I was there at the memorial, the day we met. I couldn't tell you before. I couldn't bear to speak of it.'

She held her breath, wondering if she'd done enough to ease the little girl's heart. She had her answer a moment later when Tina pulled herself free of Elena and threw herself into Alysa's arms.

'Did you love him terribly?' she whispered.

'Yes,' Alysa said quietly. 'I loved him terribly.'

'And do you love Poppa now?'

Alysa turned her head to where she could see

Drago, watching her in the doorway, his eyes full of fear and hope.

'Yes,' Alysa said. 'I love Poppa now.'

'Does Poppa love you?'

'Yes,' Drago said. 'He does.'

Tina struggled free and ran across the room to be seized up in his arms. Alysa watched them a moment before looking back at Elena, who'd folded her arms across her body, shaking.

'So you've got what you wanted,' she moaned. 'But I've lost everything.' Her wail filled the room.

'Alysa, let's get out of here,' Drago urged.

'Not yet. I still have something to do.'

She moved along the bed to where Elena was huddled, and put her arms around her.

'You haven't lost everything,' she said. 'Tina is still your granddaughter. She still loves you and she always will.'

'But *he* won't let me see her, not after this.'

'Drago won't part you from Tina,' Alysa assured her. 'He knows she needs you too, because you knew Carlotta longer than anyone.'

Elena turned suspicious eyes on Drago. 'Does she speak for you?' she demanded.

'She does,' he said gravely. 'Whatever she agrees to, I will honour.'

'You say that while she's here, but—'

'I'm going to be here for a long time,' Alysa said. 'You have nothing to fear.'

Elena looked at Drago. 'Don't hate me,' she pleaded.

'I'll never hate you,' he told her. 'You are still Tina's grandmother.' He glanced at Alysa. 'It is just as *she* says. It always will be.'

'But you'll forget Carlotta.'

'No, he won't,' Alysa said quickly. 'Carlotta will always be his real love.'

'*You* say that?'

'I'm just second best. That won't change.'

She was watching Elena, so didn't see Drago staring at her just before he carried Tina out of the room. Alysa, her heart torn with pity, gave Elena a final hug then went out to speak to Leona.

'I think she really needs to see a doctor,' she suggested.

'I know,' Leona said. 'Don't worry, she can stay with me a while, and I'll make sure she gets help.'

She looked at Alysa and Drago standing together, and gave a little nod of sad acceptance.

In the car the three of them sat together in the back seat. Tina was in her father's lap, clinging to him, eyes closed. Alysa glanced over, taking in the sight of them, contented in each other's arms, then she turned away to stare unseeingly out of the window. She needed a little time to take in what she'd done.

She had told Elena that she was coming to Italy for good, speaking on impulse with no time to consider all the implications. But they were huge. In one moment she'd tossed aside the partnership she'd striven so hard to win, and possibly her whole career. Who knew what use her qualifications would be in this country?

And she, a woman who'd always prided herself on think-ing every problem through, had done it without a moment's thought. Was she mad?

Turning slightly, she looked again at Tina and Drago, both with their eyes closed, Tina with her head against her father's chest, Drago with his head resting on his child's hair. And she knew the answer to her question.

Yes, she was mad.

Wonderfully, gloriously mad. Mad in the way only the most fortunate on earth were mad.

Heroically, blissfully mad, with the madness that lay at the heart of creation.

If her qualifications were useless here, then she would learn Italian properly and start all over from the beginning. She would do anything rather than say goodbye to Drago. No effort was beyond her, no task too great, as long as she was with him.

When had it all been decided? Long ago? Or tonight, when Drago had looked at her, imploring, putting his whole life at her mercy?

And did it matter when the decision had been made, as long as it was the right one?

As they entered Florence Tina awoke and began to look out at the streets, where the Christmas lights were still on.

'We've got lots of decorations up in the villa,' she confided to Alysa. 'And a crib. You'll like it.'

She closed her eyes again, but her hand was clutching Alysa's as though she feared to let her go.

As they reached the villa Tina opened her eyes again, looking quickly at Alysa, checking to make sure she was there.

They put her to bed together and kissed her goodnight. She was already asleep as they crept out of the room.

'What will Brian do when you don't come back?' Drago asked quietly.

'Aren't I going back?'

'You'd never have said those things to Tina if you hadn't meant them.'

'That's true.'

He led her into his own room and took her into his arms. Despite everything that had gone before, she knew that this was the first kiss of their love, the first time everything had been clear between them.

Except for one thing, her mind nudged her. But he must never know about the letter. She would keep that secret all her days, and if that meant being second best she would live with that rather than let him be hurt.

But she was strong. She would make him so happy that he would forget Carlotta. If she had still wanted revenge, that would have been the perfect way. But revenge was far from her heart now.

'Thank you for making Tina happy,' he said softly.

'Did I do the right thing?'

'You did the only thing possible to stop her heart breaking. She may have to know the truth one day, but by then she'll be strong enough to bear it.'

'I hope so,' she murmured.

'I think I knew something like this would happen, that's why I wanted you and nobody else. You see, I'd already discovered how good you were at protecting people from truths they couldn't bear.'

'What do you mean?'

'Did you think I didn't know that you did the same for me?'

She stared at him.

'The letter,' he said. 'The one in which Carlotta admitted she'd been unfaithful often before, a letter that mysteriously vanished.'

'But you—how did you—?'

'I looked in while you were reading it. I saw your face, and I saw how quickly you shoved it away to avoid showing it to me. When you'd gone to bed, I found it and I read it. Next morning it had vanished. I guessed that you'd taken it to protect me.'

'You've known since February?'

'I think in my heart I always knew about Carlotta before that, but I wouldn't admit it. I was hiding from the truth, and when I had to face it, it was almost as though something inside me grew quiet. I'd tormented myself with wondering. Now I didn't have to wonder any more, and there was a kind of peace in that.'

'I thought it would break your heart,' she said.

'And you tried to protect me, which was more than I deserved. All this time I've wondered if you'd change your mind and would tell me everything, but you never did. Last time you were here I tried to provoke you into an admission, but you held firm. I hadn't known such generosity existed. It gave me hope of winning your love.'

'How could I have let you see that letter, after what you said about clinging to your memories? It would have hurt you unbearably.'

'But you never understood my love for you, or you wouldn't have spoken of being second best. You could never be second best, don't you realise that?'

'Maybe I do now,' she whispered.

A great load had gone from her heart, leaving her free to love him totally without the slightest fear or reservation. Joy possessed her whole being.

'Could you really have gone through our life thinking of yourself as second best?' Drago asked.

Her smile was a mysterious enticement.

'If I had to,' she said. 'But there are ways to make you completely mine. I have my plans. You'll find out in time.'

'What better time than now?' he said, drawing her to the bed.

They made love drowsily, not frantic with urgency, but with the leisurely pleasure of people who knew they had all their lives. They were both tired after the long, dramatic night, but they needed this union to reaffirm that they belonged to each other heart, body and soul.

Dawn was beginning to creep around the blinds when he said, 'I need you as much as I love you. You're stronger than I am.'

'I'm stronger in some ways,' she murmured. 'You're stronger in others. It works out just fine.'

'Only if you stay with me.'

'Always—always.'

Later he said, 'When did you decide to stay?'

'When I knew that if I went back I'd have abandoned you to whatever life did to you. I couldn't do that. Would you have let me go?'

'Not for long. If this hadn't happened, I was going to call you anyway, about James. I've been doing some investigating for you. We can have him sent to England, but it would be a lot simpler to have him reburied here in a larger plot in the same cemetery. In fact…'

He seemed to become awkward and a suspicion rose in her.

'What have you done, Drago?'

'Well, you know me—the way I arrange things first and consult people afterwards, like a bulldozer. I made a few preliminary arrangements, just to get things started, and will continue only if they meet with your approval,' he finished hastily.

'What kind of preliminary arrangements?'

'I've found a good plot. He'll have a proper stone with all his details, and you can put James's photograph on it. You see, I thought—' He stopped, tongue-tied.

'Go on,' Alysa said with a little smile.

'I thought, if he was there, you'd want to visit him so you'd keep coming back. The plot isn't far from Carlotta, so even if you didn't tell me you'd arrived I could visit her at the same time and we'd bump into each other.'

'But how would you know what the right time was? Oh, of course. Silly question. You've got them all in your pocket, and there'd be a call to you as soon as I arrived. Someone would find out my hotel, and persuade me to return next day—'

'I had to find a way to lure you here if you didn't return willingly, and then— Well, it might have taken some time, but in the end you'd have realised that I was right and you belonged with me.'

'You don't even see obstacles, do you?' she demanded. 'Can I work in this country? Do my qualifications count?'

'Actually, I've been investigating that too. It's a bit complicated, but it can be done, and I know someone who'll help.'

'You're such a schemer,' she said tenderly.

'Nonsense, I just like my own way—about everything—all the time. What's wrong with that?'

She leaned close so that her hair fell on his face. 'Did you just make a joke?'

'I don't know. Did I?'

'It had better have been a joke.'

'Don't pretend to be alarmed. You do what you like with me, and you know it.'

She laughed and kissed him.

'I guess Tina was right about you.'

'She told you I was a softy, didn't she? I got it out of her in the end. It cost me a few cream buns—and a new doll, and some shoes, and books about her favourite cartoon character, and I forget the rest, but she drove a hard bargain.'

'Her father's daughter,' Alysa mused.

They laughed and embraced, but after a moment she said, 'I'll have to go back to England and work out my notice. I can't just let them down.'

'I know you won't do that.'

'I'll be here for Christmas, and every weekend until my notice is over.'

'Just promise to return here finally, and become my wife. I'm a patient man, beloved. I've waited for you this long. I can wait a little longer, if I know that you'll be mine in the end. As you were always meant to be.'

Two days before Christmas Eve the weather turned nasty. Planes were delayed, and those waiting for loved ones lingered anxiously at airports.

'She should be here by now, Poppa,' Tina

said anxiously, staring out of the window into the black sky.

'The board says the plane will be late, *cara*. We just have to be patient.'

'But she will come, won't she?'

And just for a moment the little girl was back in time, waiting for her mother's return, waiting, waiting…

Drago heard the echo and quickly dropped down beside her.

'Of course she's coming, darling. It's only the weather.'

'But there could be an accident?'

'No, look up there.' He pointed up to the sky where lights had just appeared in the distance. 'There's a plane coming in now.'

Let it be Alysa's, he prayed silently. Beside him he could feel that Tina was tense as both of them kept their eyes on the incoming lights.

Down they came, lower and lower, until the plane touched the ground, screaming away down the runway, out of sight until it could turn and taxi back.

Let it be hers—let it be hers.

'Poppa, look!'

Tina was pointing up at the board where against the London flight the red 'delayed' had changed to the green of 'landed'.

'She's here, she's here!' Tina was dancing with excitement.

Drago grinned broadly, wishing he could join her.

They hurried to the barrier to greet her, and at the first glimpse Tina rushed away, hauling her father after her.

'You're home, you're home!' she squealed.

'Yes,' she said softly, her eyes on Drago. 'I'm home.'

Drago's driver had almost gone to sleep waiting, but he roused and greeted her with a wave as they exited the airport hand in hand.

They all sat in the back of the car. Alysa took Tina onto her lap, wrapping her in her arms while the little girl babbled happily on their way to the villa.

'Look, it's snowing really hard.'

'So I see,' Alysa said, gazing out of the window to where the white flakes filled the air. 'I'm glad that waited until I landed.'

'Was it a bumpy flight?' Drago asked.

'A bit, and I'm not a good flyer. But I just kept

thinking about what was waiting for me here— both of you, and the future we'll all have.' She met Drago's eyes again. 'The journey can be easy if you know what journey's end will be.'

She knew, because Drago had told her in a phone call two days ago, that this journey's end would include a meeting with the head of a local accountancy firm who had 'matters to discuss' with her. She was looking forward to that. Brian had been more reasonable than she'd dared to hope, and her release might be in as soon as six weeks. For this the ambitious Frank could take some credit, having avidly scooped up her clients in a way that had reminded Alysa of herself as she had once been.

The other person who would be waiting for her in the villa was Elena.

'I promised her that she wouldn't be shut out,' Drago had explained on the phone.

'And this is the perfect time to prove it,' she'd agreed.

'The thing is, she doesn't seem able to accept reassurance from me. It has to be you.'

'How is Tina with her? Does she seem frightened after what happened?'

'Strangely enough, no. I explained to her that Nonna wasn't well because she was so unhappy about Carlotta, and Tina understood at once. Now, as well as mothering me, she mothers Elena. Give her half a chance, she'll start mothering you.'

Now, as they drove up to the villa, Alysa could see Elena's pale, anxious face looking through a window, and she knew what she had to do—not only for Elena, but for Tina, who was watching closely.

So she burst into the house with a happy smile on her face, her arms thrown wide in greeting, and had her reward in Elena's look of passionate relief as they hugged each other. There was no more to be said.

'Now it's time you were in bed,' Drago told Tina.

'Please, Poppa, let me show Alysa the crib first?'

'I'd like to see it,' she said.

It was there, dominating the hall. Unlike the one she'd had two years ago, it was an expensive creation, but there at its heart was the same beauty and simplicity. Mary sat by the crib, her face radiant and tender as she watched over her child, while Joseph stood just behind, never taking his eyes from the two creatures that were his to love and protect.

'He's just been born,' Tina explained. 'And Mary is so happy that she has him.' She added confidingly, 'Mamma told me that.'

'And he's happy too,' Alysa said softly. 'Because he has his mother, and they make a family, even though—' she spoke carefully '—he has another family as well. Because you can love more than one person, even more than one mother.'

'Yes,' Tina said firmly.

'Now it's time for you to go to bed,' Drago said. 'We've got a big day tomorrow, with lots of shopping to do.'

'Why don't you ask Nonna to take you up?' Alysa said, indicating Elena.

They watched the old woman and the child climbing the stairs together, contented again in each other's company.

'I was afraid Tina might not be able to accept me,' Alysa said in wonder. 'But she did, from the first moment.'

'She looked at you and just knew that we all belong together,' Drago agreed. 'A family. The kind of family I never dared to hope for again.

Alysa, my love, my dearest, my future. Do you believe in miracles?'

'I believe in this one,' she answered at once in a voice so fervent that it was almost a prayer. 'And I believe in all the others that we're going to make together. I love you, and I believe you love me. I believe that your love will be with me for all eternity. And that is the greatest miracle of all.'

MILLS & BOON PUBLISH EIGHT LARGE PRINT TITLES A MONTH. THESE ARE THE EIGHT TITLES FOR APRIL 2009.

— ఴ —

THE GREEK TYCOON'S DISOBEDIENT BRIDE
Lynne Graham

THE VENETIAN'S MIDNIGHT MISTRESS
Carole Mortimer

RUTHLESS TYCOON, INNOCENT WIFE
Helen Brooks

THE SHEIKH'S WAYWARD WIFE
Sandra Marton

THE ITALIAN'S CHRISTMAS MIRACLE
Lucy Gordon

CINDERELLA AND THE COWBOY
Judy Christenberry

HIS MISTLETOE BRIDE
Cara Colter

PREGNANT: FATHER WANTED
Claire Baxter

MILLS & BOON

Pure reading pleasure™

MILLS & BOON PUBLISH EIGHT LARGE PRINT TITLES A MONTH. THESE ARE THE EIGHT TITLES FOR MAY 2009.

———————— ❧ ————————

THE BILLIONAIRE'S BRIDE OF VENGEANCE
Miranda Lee

THE SANTANGELI MARRIAGE
Sara Craven

THE SPANIARD'S VIRGIN HOUSEKEEPER
Diana Hamilton

THE GREEK TYCOON'S RELUCTANT BRIDE
Kate Hewitt

NANNY TO THE BILLIONAIRE'S SON
Barbara McMahon

CINDERELLA AND THE SHEIKH
Natasha Oakley

PROMOTED: SECRETARY TO BRIDE!
Jennie Adams

THE BLACK SHEEP'S PROPOSAL
Patricia Thayer

MILLS & BOON®
Pure reading pleasure™